One Aladdin Two Lamps

ALSO BY JEANETTE WINTERSON

NOVELS

Oranges Are Not the Only Fruit
The Passion
Sexing the Cherry
Written on the Body
Art & Lies
Gut Symmetries

The Powerbook
Lighthousekeeping
The Stone Gods
The Gap of Time
Frankissstein: A Love Story

SHORT STORIES

The World and Other Places
Christmas Days: 12 Stories and 12

Feasts for 12 Days
Night Side of the River

NOVELLAS

Weight (Myth)
The Daylight Gate (Horror)

NON-FICTION

Art Objects: Essays in Ecstasy and Effrontery
Courage Calls to Courage Everywhere

12 Bytes: How Artificial Intelligence Will Change the Way We Live and Love

MEMOIR

Why Be Happy When You Could Be Normal?

COLLABORATIONS

Land (with Antony Gormley and Clare Richardson)

CHILDREN'S BOOKS

Tanglewreck
The Lion, the Unicorn and Me

The King of Capri
The Battle of the Sun

COMIC BOOKS

Boating for Beginners

One Aladdin Two Lamps

JEANETTE WINTERSON

JONATHAN CAPE
LONDON

1 3 5 7 9 10 8 6 4 2

Jonathan Cape, an imprint of Vintage, is part of the
Penguin Random House group of companies

Vintage, Penguin Random House UK, One Embassy
Gardens, 8 Viaduct Gardens, London SW11 7BW

penguin.co.uk/vintage
global.penguinrandomhouse.com

First published by Jonathan Cape in 2025

Copyright © Jeanette Winterson 2025

The moral right of the author has been asserted

Every effort has been made to trace copyright holders and to obtain their permission. The publisher apologises for any errors or omissions and, if notified of any corrections, will make suitable acknowledgment in future reprints or editions of this book.

Penguin Random House values and supports copyright. Copyright fuels creativity, encourages diverse voices, promotes freedom of expression and supports a vibrant culture. Thank you for purchasing an authorised edition of this book and for respecting intellectual property laws by not reproducing, scanning or distributing any part of it by any means without permission. You are supporting authors and enabling Penguin Random House to continue to publish books for everyone. No part of this book may be used or reproduced in any manner for the purpose of training artificial intelligence technologies or systems. In accordance with Article 4(3) of the DSM Directive 2019/790, Penguin Random House expressly reserves this work from the text and data mining exception.

Typeset in 12.5/15.2pt Garamond Premier Pro by Six Red Marbles UK, Thetford, Norfolk
Printed and bound in Great Britain by Clays Ltd, Elcograf S.p.A.

The authorised representative in the EEA is Penguin Random House Ireland,
Morrison Chambers, 32 Nassau Street, Dublin D02 YH68

A CIP catalogue record for this book is available from the British Library

ISBN 9781787336124

Penguin Random House is committed to a sustainable future
for our business, our readers and our planet. This book
is made from Forest Stewardship Council® certified paper.

For Philippa Brewster. 1949–2024. My first publisher, sometime lover, always friend.

I'm telling you stories. Trust me.

The Passion, 1987

START HERE

Morning. Crisp as an apple.
Where are we?
On the street.
Here? In this city?
No. Another place.
When? Now?
Not now. Many years ago.
What are we doing here?
We're going to see a pantomime.

There's a snake of children wrapped around the theatre front to back.
It's eleven o'clock in the morning. The factory where my dad works has decided to take all the workers' children to a show at Christmas time.

I'm wearing a duffle coat and a pair of borrowed shiny patent shoes. I don't know anyone. My dad works in another town and rides his bike to the factory. All weathers. He can't afford the bus. Today is frosty and clear. I am cold in these shoes.

Inside, the small theatre has red velvet seats raked in front of the stage. The carpet is a swirl of acanthus leaves. The smell is toffee and Vimto.

I am on my own at the back. There's a sandwich in my pocket. Breakfast. Eat it.

Above the swagged curtains, there's a plaster medallion of Queen Victoria. She looks down in disapproval at the squabbling rows of jostling kids.

The yelling stops. None of us has ever been to a theatre before.

The curtains are opening.

Where are we?

Peking. A washhouse. Sheets piled up like snowdrifts. An angry mother shoots her head over a pile. Aladdin! Where are you? You lazy, good-for-nothing, hopeless, daydreaming-come-to-a-bad-end boy!

Aladdin is cross-legged on top of a tower of bright blue pillows. He's reading.

The Story of Aladdin and His Wonderful Lamp is Britain's favourite pantomime. This tale, from China, via India and Persia, arrived with the Empire, in the early 1800s, with the fascination for all things Oriental. The Victorians loved it, shaping it to their own values. Rags to Riches. Poor Boy Makes Good. Hard Work Wins the Day.

Most of us know the story of Aladdin from Disney movies and the musical. The text is stranger, certainly because the story travelled mouth to mouth, before it was written down, and people have a way of adding what they want and losing what they don't. It looks like a Hero story, but that's not the truth of it.

Aladdin is a series of encounters. The outcomes are not fixed. The setbacks and reversals of fortune that make us cheer and boo are more than comedy turns. They tell a truth about human chances, about the enmeshing of character and circumstances. This is a story, and the glory of stories is that they change.

Ten years later, I was walking to the library to return a book. A collection of tales called *The Arabian Nights*.
That version was only the few stories that everyone in the West knows so well. Sinbad the Sailor. Aladdin and his Magic Lamp. Ali Baba and the Forty Thieves. The Fisherman and the Genie. I was hoping to discover the whereabouts of a magic lamp. Or a flying carpet. Anything to help me escape.
The stained glass window in the Accrington Public Library said *Industry and Prudence Conquer*.
This was a Carnegie library, paid for by the Scottish steel magnate, Andrew Carnegie, who had gone to America, made a fortune, and endowed libraries all over the world.
This was how the story was supposed to go. Work hard. Do well.
But . . .
I am female. I am adopted. I felt more like Aladdin than Andrew Carnegie. A lifetime of hard work would never get me out of here. I was trapped in a story I didn't want to hear.

The librarian was interested that I was interested in tales from the East. She told me there was a complete text of the *Nights* in the Oriental Section. That was in the days when ordinary libraries in ordinary towns had an Oriental Section.
I opened the book.

One Thousand and One Nights begins with an ending. An ending that is intended to run on repeat until the world is dead.

*

There's a Sultan called Shahryar.

He discovers that both he and his brother have wives who have been extravagantly unfaithful. We're not talking about a lover in the afternoon. No, these were toyboys of every shape, colour and size – and all at once. The fact that the two kings enjoyed harems decorated with wives and concubines is irrelevant. In this world women belong to men. Possessions must not have a life of their own.

To avenge himself, and men the world over, Sultan Shahryar decrees he will wed a fresh virgin every night and murder her every morning. That way, she won't have a chance to cheat. Order is restored.

Understandably, the Kingdom is running out of virgins. The Sultan's adviser, the Grand Vizier, happens to have two he keeps at home, and so far, they have been spared. The eldest is called Shahrazad. In the West, we call her Scheherazade.

Shahrazad freely offers herself as the Sultan's next bride, by which we mean virgin sacrifice, and her father is unable to dissuade her by threats or promises.

As the Sultan brings Shahrazad to his bed, before the ritual beheading that will take place in the morning, his overnight bride starts to tell a story. The Sultan is intrigued, and as the story is still in tale by daybreak, Shahrazad is allowed to live another day – and night – and day and night, every story opening into another story, so that there is no time to die.

One Thousand and One Nights began as stories to be told round the campfire, or in the market, or crossing the desert, or in the cool of the evening. Like all stories that pass from mouth to mouth and hand to hand, they changed over time. New stories were tacked onto the skirts of old favourites.

Fresh characters appeared. Popular latecomers like Aladdin and Ali Baba got their own mini-series within the whole. There was no rush. It took, perhaps, four hundred years for the earliest tales known in India and Persia, in the 8th century, to join with later stories from Iraq in the 9th century, and onwards still, gathering fables from Egypt and Syria, until something like what we are reading now was caught together in one place, firstly in Arabic, and then in translation – the translations themselves bringing in new variants.

Stories have a way of escaping. Recombining. Defying neatness.

The untidy exuberance of these stories – taking their character from where they land, finding their way through geography and history, mobilising different cultures and customs to extend their reach, cleverly settling wherever they are received, before moving on – is emblematic of humanity itself. No other species adapts to everywhere and anywhere. Hot or cold. Harsh or fertile. Sea and land. That is the human success story. Multiple. Teeming. Expansive. Inventive. Ceaseless.

Alf Layla Wa-Layla. One Thousand and One Nights is an overflowing bazaar of such stories: moral and immoral, by turns bloodthirsty and forgiving, bawdy and pious, accepting magic as part of everyday life, understanding, without the need for explanation, that the visible human world is only a part of the mostly invisible bigger world. In this larger world, different life forms living on different planes collide with human endeavour – for good and ill.

*

Life expectancy is core to the stories as it is core to the storyteller.

Non-biological beings are not subject to time as mortals are – they can live long, perhaps forever. The misalignment between human and non-human experiences of time is part of the comedy, and sometimes the tragedy, of these tales – especially so, as the tales are told by a woman whose life is in the measure of an hourglass.

Her only hope is to dispute the fixity of time.

Every night Shahrazad gains another day. She frees herself from her Time Lord by going into battle against Time itself.

And she succeeds. The single night allotted to her by the Sultan swells to a thousand more. And then, onwards, into a future whose beats cannot be counted.

Shahrazad succeeds because she understands that beginnings, middles and ends are only useful when we are working in chronological time – the arrow flight of the day, or the marks that chart the month. Inner time, where our minds live, where we daydream and create, where children play, is not subject to chronological imperatives.

In recognition of this, the stories humans tell have always compressed and expanded time, can fit a life into a single day, unravel a single day into strings that become an instrument – not of measurement, but of music.

We can begin at the end. Or in the middle. We can enjoy multiple beginnings – and see what happens.

The story unfolds in time, just as we do, but not in time as we commonly experience it. In a few hours we can live many lifetimes. More importantly, the freedom from daily time that the story allows, points us towards the strange truth of our hybrid nature:

We are mortal but we must live as though we are not.

Shahrazad's genius is to recognise that while her pressing problem sits inside chronological time – *in the morning she will die* – her solution lies beyond the limits of ordinary time.

Her method is to dismantle the Sultan's ticking madness and replace it with the sanity of a story. A story where a year can pass in two seconds and where there is no need to worry about one lifetime when many more are available to us.

Shahrazad refuses the present emergency – the contrived drama of a powerful man. Instead, she rolls out time like a flying carpet. A means of escape. She does not lie weeping on the divan, counting the moments until her death; instead she invites the Sultan to travel with her on a leisurely journey to somewhere more interesting.

Where are we going?

To the desert to meet a man who is in a mess through no fault of his own.

It is possible to open what is closed. To dodge what seems inevitable. To stretch what is shrunk. To counter one story with another.

Walking back from the library, town at the bottom and a hill at the top, a town that might as well have been a walled fortress, set inside a moat guarded by crocodiles, my heart was light. I had found my magic lamp and flying carpet.

Let's put it like this.

I can change the story because I am the story.

THE STORY

A merchant sits down to eat his lunch.
Hot day. Long travels. Gentle oasis. Camels calm. Lean back. Relax.

The aubergine is tasty. The bread is satisfying. Cool water for his tongue and feet. And his wife has packed his favourite dates.

The merchant is dreaming of a time that's not this time. Not here and now. Another place. Life will be easier there. Until then, and for now, he will sleep until the heat is softer. Afterwards, walk on. He must go on. Today, tomorrow, the next day. Life is as it is.

The merchant stands up, stretches, finishes one last delicious date, and throws away the stone.

The stone hits an invisible being who happens to be passing by. The missile kills the being (stone) dead. The merchant has no idea of this. He's just eating his lunch and daydreaming.

What's that dust cloud on the horizon? Why is it coming this way?

The merchant lies down behind his camels and covers his head with a sack.

No use.

The cloud solidifies. Is it a jinn? Is it a jinnia?

The merchant peeks from under the sack. He trembles. His sweat smells worse than camel dung.

An Ifrit stands before him, glaring down over the humpty camels. This is not good. Jinn can be reasonable. Or friendly. Or curious like cats. They jump down to earth to take a look at what's going on. Ifrits are bigger, meaner, madder, winged, and although they too live in the air, outrage is their natural element.

This Ifrit is no different to his kind. Outraged, he beats his breast and stamps his feet and claims a life for a life. The merchant protests that it was an accident, and how can anyone hope to kill, or save, a being they cannot see?

And the lethal properties of date stones? Who knew?

No use.

The Ifrit roars like the eye of the tiger.

The merchant might not be to blame, not exactly, but he must pay the price. A life for a life. That's the rule.

Pleading yields no mercy, but the Ifrit is bound by the laws of Allah, and the merchant has a last request which the Ifrit must grant.

'Ifrit! Grant me one year to travel home and put my affairs in order. I wish to settle my debts, take leave of my tearful wife, and provide for my unhappy children.'

The Ifrit folds its leg of mutton arms across its bare bull chest.

'Merchant! Your request is granted according to the Will of Allah. Return to this spot, in one year and one day, to forfeit your life.'

The merchant starts loading his camels. The Ifrit spins himself into a cloud of self-satisfied dust. He's gone.

The merchant knows there is no escape.

Who can escape their fate?

I CAN CHANGE
THE STORY.
I AM THE STORY.

That is the beginning of the first story Shahrazad tells the Sultan. It turns out to be a story about a man whose life is saved by a story.
Should this surprise us?
Think how many lives are lost to the 'wrong' story.

I am poor. I am a woman. I am queer. I am non-white. I am uneducated. I am plain. I am shy. I am ill. I am an only child. I am a single parent. I am unemployed. I live in my brother's shadow. My mother never loved me. My father abused me. I am an immigrant. I am . . . what?

The facts of our lives seem to bind us fast. There's a narrative that starts before we are born. Is your Daddy rich? Is your Momma good-looking? Will the living be easy?

For the lucky ones, there might be the 'right' story. Loving parents, stable home, nice school, opportunities, friends. Then, later on, money and self-direction. A life of chances.

But what if we are not so fortunate?

Before we can speak for ourselves, our circumstances are creating the self that will speak. Our lines are being written by others. The world out there starts to shape us. To shape our developing minds.

Who Am I? What Am I?

Most of us, I think, understand the importance of environment and upbringing. The situation in which we find ourselves, and with whom – our micro-world – that's the world that starts to fire and wire the neurons in the baby brain. And just beyond the arms that hold us (or don't) and the parent(s) who feed(s) us, is the effect of the macro-world. Is there a war on? Bombs falling? Is there famine? Are we with our mother waiting for the aid truck? Do we live in a dictatorship or a democracy? Does our family feel safe?

The Nurture story is a lottery – we don't get to choose our parents. We don't get to choose the world we're born into.

The Nature story seems even more fixed and immutable. You can run away from your family or your country, maybe you can escape a war, but you can't run away from your DNA.

Is that right?

Some people are born taller, prettier, stronger than others. Some seem to have a natural talent, or an inclination towards a skill or a sport, long before anyone teaches them. Are you 'a chip off the old block'? Were you 'born this way'? My mother, Mrs Winterson, had a typically bleak version of this – because I am adopted, and therefore she couldn't be blamed for my badness – 'What's bred in the bone comes out in the marrow.'

Since Charles Darwin's *On the Origin of Species* (1859), closely followed by his cousin Francis Galton's musings, *Hereditary Genius* (1869), the lure of characteristics inborn and inbred has been fashionable – and fatalistic.

Charles Darwin was a scientific genius. He was also a Victorian patriarch. He believed that women were physically and mentally 'inferior' to men, and while he was against slavery on moral grounds, and aware that 'race' is far more of a social construct than a biological reality, he wrote in *The Descent of Man* (1871) that the 'civilised races would almost certainly obliterate and replace the savage races'.

It's an example of Science Darwin, the fieldwork, evidence-based biologist, versus Story Darwin. His discoveries are sound science. He knew that creationism was a story that needed to be rewritten; he never understood that the *Boy's Own* tropes of Empire were inventions masquerading as fact.

Francis Galton used Darwin's sound science to underpin his own unscientific narrative. It was he who coined the term 'eugenics'.

It means Good Genes.

Galton advocated the sterilisation and eventual elimination of 'undesirables', along with the equivalent of a livestock programme for humans. All we would be doing is speeding up nature's slow sifting process. Get rid of the weak. Encourage the strong. We know where those views led – the Nazis were as enthusiastic about the gas chambers as they were about a pure and superior Aryan race.

Backing up Francis Galton was the philosopher Herbert Spencer. Spencer took it upon himself to sum up *On the Origin of Species* as Survival of the Fittest. That is some of what Darwin was saying – and by the fifth reprint, he had included the famous line. The trouble is, turning a complex thesis into a tabloid headline soon became, and continues to be, to this day, the take-away science-y soundbite for the justification of any oppression you care to choose: racism, sexism, slavery, the class system.

Those who worried that evolution was an affront to creationism were soothed by the likes of Galton and Spencer philosophising that the outcomes of both systems were aligned.

> *The rich man in his castle / The poor man at his gate / God made them high or lowly / and ordered their estate.*

So goes a favourite hymn of 1848, 'All Things Bright and Beautiful'. Poor children in Sunday schools learned this off by heart. One hundred and twenty years later, I was that poor child, still singing it off by heart.

Survival of the Fittest – natural selection – is a secular version of God's Chosen People. The best rise 'naturally' to the top, in what 19th-century biologists loved to call 'the struggle for existence'.

Certainly, humanoid life has had to struggle to survive over the 300,000 years or so of our time on earth. Predators, weather, food scarcity, disease. Mental terror. Neanderthals. Yet, since the beginning of what we call civilisation, only about 6,000 years ago, how much of that 'struggle' is of our own making is worth the calculation.

Humans (I would say male ones but you might disagree and I would listen) are addicted to war, no matter how worthless and ruinous. All of us, it seems, are unable to refrain from waging war on our one true home: this planet.

We have learned how to manage the forces of Nature, but we cannot manage ourselves.

*

Galton, Spencer, and the supporters of Survival of the Fittest as a social doctrine, were sincere in wanting to breed a better, fitter race.

Eugenics, they believed, would end poverty and misery, engineering strong and productive citizens. They rejected the social democracy solutions of the French Revolution (1789) with its Liberty, Equality, Fraternity, and they particularly disliked the theories of Jean-Jacques Rousseau, whose essay competition entry, *Discourse on the Origin and Foundation of Inequality Among Men* (1754), became the central text that spurred the Revolution.

Darwin's younger friend, the palaeontologist Thomas Huxley, wrote of Rousseau: 'The doctrine that all men are... free and equal, is an utterly baseless fiction.'

It's interesting that Huxley's grandson, Aldous, wrote *Brave New World* (1932), showing us a future where social democracy had failed, and where genetic engineering had won the argument. In that Utopia, no one is equal, or free; work and leisure hierarchies are fixed, but everyone is batch-hatched to be happy.

A year after *Brave New World* was published, Adolf Hitler became Chancellor of Germany. Theories of racial superiority and ethnic cleansing found a brutal champion.

Those utterly baseless theories are staging a comeback around the world as we move into the second quarter of the 21st century.

Such theories have never gone away, of course, but Fascism made them repellent. After 1945, the social, racial, gender-essentialist 'natural' hierarchies that dominated our past have been progressively challenged. The world that has opened up, since then, was for many – for women, for working people, for people of colour – a fairer world.

I have written 'was' and not 'is' because much of the West is at an existential crossroads.

The far right is open about its own desire – and what it believes to be its popular mandate – to return society to what it describes as traditional values. Nationalism. Hard borders. Faith. Family. Flag. Gender roles that conform to pre-feminist expectations.

Right-wingers, women, as well as men, lament what feminism has done to the family. What too many women with college degrees will do to the male ego. What too many immigrants will do to a country (pick one). What will happen to children if drag queens or trans folk read them stories. Often the question is left dangling, so anyone who feels any unease around progress can fill in their own horror show.

None of this would matter too much if the time we lived in was not the amplified age of the internet, where millions of followers will cluster round ideas rotten at the core – like flies on a carcass.

One click over a lunchtime sandwich will take you to whatever trans-national pit of grievance-filled armchair-avengers attracts your own brand of darkness.

Zombie science is back with a bang.

Is IQ race-based? Is IQ genetic? Born stupid die stupid. Are men 'naturally' superior to women? Are white men better than black men at responsibility and leadership? Is America being flooded with 'bad genes'? Nobody needs to search for a late-night Shock Jock radio station. This stuff is everywhere.

Race is the petrol-bomb, but all progressive policies are

now threatened by radical-rightwing thuggery. For me, what's happening around women's rights – abortion, employment, equality, independence and gender roles – is especially disturbing. This isn't niche stuff. Women make up more than half the population of the world.

Equality seems to upset the radical-right. In the USA, DEI hires are now legislated against, with a view to forcing similar compliance from European companies who trade with America.

Opponents of equality of race, class and gender are back to speaking openly about what they claim are 'natural' hierarchies, either God-given and driven, or genetic.

Where, they ask, online, or on their talk shows, is the historical evidence for equality of mind, when non-white 'races', or women, have contributed so little, apart from useful labour, to benefit literature, or philosophy, or science, or invention, or politics, or the arts? Civilisation is white. It's Greek. It's Roman. It's European. It's male. Women can join in, but the game, and its rules, are man-made. And that's because in real life, some people (historically, northern European white males) are just better fitted for the Job.

It may not be Woke, they claim, but it's True.

Is it true?

The Western colonialist view of benighted savages civilised by the White Man is impossible to support. Impossible that is, if you prefer facts to self-soothing fictions.

Africa is where modern humans begin – every person alive can trace their genetic ancestry to Africa. That's why all humans share 99.9 per cent of our DNA. Why are we so different to one another, culturally, religiously? That's Nurture not Nature. Where you are born, and into what, and with whom, is what makes the difference. Not the 0.1 per cent of DNA difference.

Africa. The mother of us all.

Far from being the 'dark continent' as the British named it, Africa, in its hugeness and abundance, developed its own cultures, kingdoms, politics and trade routes, without Western input or interference. In many parts of that vast continent, non-centralised governance was the people's choice – a progressive choice that Western societies are at last beginning to rediscover for themselves. Alongside non-centralised governance, vast empires of the hierarchical kind the West prefers, developed in Ethiopia (Christian) and Mali (Muslim).

Founded in the mid-1200s, the Kingdom of Mali became one of the largest empires in the world for more than 300 years – multi-ethnic, multi-lingual, with Islam as the dominant religion, and with around 50 million subjects and a land mass bigger than western Europe. Its centres of learning included Timbuktu, where astronomers, engineers and architects created astonishing buildings, often cosmically aligned, like the Great Mosque, a clay building finished around 1325 and a UNESCO world heritage site.

(Fun fact: Notre Dame in Paris was completed in 1345. It's also a UNESCO world heritage site.)

Mali's Sankore University was fully staffed at that time, and it included the largest library in Africa, with close to a million manuscripts. The Portuguese, who first visited there in the early 16th century, have left ample records of the empire's scholarly and civilised society. And its gold reserves.

All empires fall, and Mali was no different, but the history of West Africa is not a history of illiterates in loincloths waiting to work on tobacco and sugar plantations belonging to the White Man.

And the scale of enslavement is worth a moment's pause. Between 1500 and 1866, the Trans-Atlantic Slave Trade Database estimates that 12.5 million Africans were taken. That's a lot of people unable to make their contribution to anything but crop picking.

Yet, when North Africans colonised the Iberian peninsula, starting in the 8th century, founding the great city of Córdoba, they imported wisdom and culture from the ancient world in Arabic translations – medicine, chemistry, philosophy, astronomy – and they brought with them practical knowledge learned out of Egypt, including tumbler locks and keys, and drainage and irrigation systems that were feats of engineering, especially a 2,000-mile series of canals and basins designed to bring water down from the Sierra Nevada to farms, villages and towns. It's a system still in use today, and a model for sustainable agriculture.

Most of us, in the Western world, are taught that we have the Greeks to thank for mathematics, overlooking Egyptian and Sumerian systems, but also the fact that it was Indian mathematicians who introduced zero as a mathematical number and concept. The Greeks worked with one to nine.

India invented the decimal system. What we still call Arabic numerals is the simplified mathematical system adopted by the Moors from North Africa, via India, and brought to Spain.

The truth of the world, its peoples, its cultures, its art and inventions, is so much richer and more fascinating than white exceptionalism allows.

From China, it was not only gunpowder, porcelain and silk that transformed the world economy, and opened up the famous silk roads that linked trade of all kinds between East and West; it's the compass, the mechanical clock – the early moveable type – long before Europe got in on the game. And while we are on games, both chess and snakes and ladders originated in India, while Mahjong and Go came from China. We have Go to thank for giving software engineers a platform to develop the skill of Google's DeepMind programme, AlphaGo.

I could go on . . . and on . . . and we would soon be neck-down in Western colonisation and slavery, into the Opium Wars, into the jingoism of Empire, enforced religion, the White Man's burden, the necessary fictions people live by, so that they can sleep at night.

In 2002, Boris Johnson, a journalist who was never concerned about the lines between fact and fiction (or do I mean truth and lies?) and who eventually became British prime minister on the back of Brexit, claimed that Africa was a 'blot', but not a blot on the British conscience. Its problems were nothing to do with the evils of the slave trade, any colonial legacy, or IMF debt-loading. No. None of that.

Africa's issue, declared Johnson, was not that Britain had been in charge, but that Britain is no longer in charge. He then riffed on 'natives' eating plantain, instead of planting tobacco, coffee and cotton (crops to sell cheap to Western creditors).

That's the kind of fact-free history that supremacy narratives depend on.

Certainly, the typical Western education system is one that relies on out-of-date narratives it calls 'lessons'. Attempts to correct these out-of-date and misleading narratives always meet with objections from 'traditionalists'. The 1619 Project, in the USA, was called unpatriotic by many on the right of American politics, including Donald Trump. Simply, it was a different way of reading American history – and one that put enslaved Africans at the centre of the story.

Any writer will tell you that if you change the centre of a story, that shift of emphasis automatically affects the beginning, and likely the end.

Think about that.

The centre of the story might not be anything as obvious as 'what happens'. It might be the central idea, or ideology. In the same way that Darwin, the storyteller, could not conceive of a way of telling his story without the narrative nets thrown over his mind by patriarchy and Empire, so do we all, in ways great and small, fit the facts to our fictions.

A good example would be Richard Dawkins' *The Selfish Gene* (1976), hugely important in its reconceptualisation of what a gene is, and, therefore, what biological life is. The title though, is misleading, even Dawkins thinks so, because the story isn't about 'selfishness' at all – not in the way we commonly use and understand that word

Yet the title is attractive because it keys with Darwin's Survival of the Fittest, and locks nicely to the presently dominant world-think that tells the human story as necessarily and *naturally* violent, ruthless, competitive, capitalist, might-is-right, Me First struggle for existence that says: I win. You lose. Winner takes all.

People who haven't read Dawkins' book misconstrue it to their pet fictional theory; we're all selfish bastards, just like our genes.

The facts are the facts. They stay as they are. The story is the thing that moves.

Stories matter.

And if deconstructing the heart of a story will alter its beginnings, think how this might apply to how we understand the world.

Here's a simple example.

When you were learning algebra at school, did your teacher begin by explaining that this word is, in fact, al-Jabr, which means to reunite what is broken – in mathematics, to restore balance to an equation?

Did she begin by explaining how algebra developed in the Muslim Arabic world in the 9th century?

And would it be interesting to spend that lesson looking at both East and West, to wonder how numbers and symbols have been understood and interpreted by very different cultures, both practically and conceptually?

Islam forbids representational images of Allah and the prophets, because of the belief that the spiritual can't be defined by the literal. This view fits perfectly with the mathematical advancement of representing numbers by symbols.

So, kids could begin to learn algebra, on Day One, as a window on the world. As an example of how different people in different places with different priorities might think – and therefore what they might spend their time thinking *about*.

Sure, the kids will have to buckle down and do the maths, but nothing sits in isolation, and shouldn't. So much of learning seems pointless and arbitrary to children but would not if it were connected to life itself – if learning was about more than acquiring whatever basics you need for a job. That shift can't happen unless all learning is understood as the study of human thought. Whether it's music or maths, French or physics, Humanities or STEM, because even the most basic fact comes with a story attached. And stories reflect the concerns of the storyteller. No story is neutral or objective. That doesn't make stories unreliable – they are reliably the record of difference and change. The damage we do, the *evil* we do, is when we twist the facts to fit our warped storytelling. When we don't, or won't, realise that we are interpreting facts according to whatever is the current fashionable fiction. When we claim that Our Story is The Story.

When the teacher has explained about Islamic Persia, she can move on to the timeline of computing science – which will get her on to working-class hero, George Boole, without whom your smartphone wouldn't work. He wasn't a member of the 19th-century leisured, or privileged, class of males whose education was paid for out of family funds. His father was a shoemaker. George taught himself algebra.

And George had an interesting acquaintance who will

carry the lesson right into feminism. She was a member of that vast body of people whose potential went unrecognised, and whose history was overlooked as trivial.

Women.

George's fellow (the language we have to use!) mathematician was Ada Byron, later Countess Lovelace (1815–52).

Ada Lovelace was the world's first computer programmer for a machine that didn't exist.

In Ada's day, and long before, and for some time afterwards, most women were not educated beyond the basics, if they were educated at all. Women were there to raise children, manage the home, be decorative and, depending on their social status, undertake low-paid work or marry the breadwinner.

Ada was educated, and she was educated in maths – unheard of at the time for a woman. This was not because her family was progressive; it was to prevent her from going mad. Her father was Britain's most famous poet, Lord Byron. The man his lover Caroline Lamb, described as 'mad, bad, and dangerous to know'. Byron didn't want his daughter studying what he considered to be an explosive occupation with serious mental health consequences – at least for women. What was it?

Poetry.

Maths it had to be, then.

Ada's unique and bizarre personal history allowed her to befriend Charles Babbage – an independently wealthy, privately educated upper-class male – who was always building a machine-type-computer-type thing, but not quite. This was at a time when tedious calculations for engineering, and for sea voyages, had to be worked out by hand – by human 'computers' as they were called. These computers were often women who pretended their husbands did the job.

Ada was much more interested in the possibilities that might be opened up by such a machine than by the machine itself. Programming it, in her mind, in 1840, Ada had this to say:

> *By the word operation we mean any process that alters the mutual relation between two or more things. This is the most general definition and would include all subjects in the universe.*

All subjects in the universe? That's a long way past number crunching.

Ada was imagining a computing future that would develop beyond sequencing numbers. It was Ada's maths tutor, Augustus De Morgan, who introduced Ada to the work of George Boole. Boole pushed the discoveries of algebra forward into what we understand as Symbolic Logic – the basis of digital computer circuits. Boole never got the level of recognition he deserved in his lifetime, and Ada got no recognition at all.

Imagine if Ada and George had been voted in as a job-share for the Lucasian Professorship of Mathematics at Cambridge, along with Babbage, who held the post. But women were not allowed to hold professorships. Or hold anything much at all. Except a baby.

When I read about Ada Lovelace, such a lone star, I

recognise that she was a gifted individual, but I wonder too, how scientific and cultural and philosophical and political advancement would have been different, if all women, not just the lone stars, had been allowed to measure themselves on equal terms with men?

Those upper-class women who were educated, were educated at home with a tutor. They had no opportunity for lively discussions with other students and tutors. They were not admitted to the professions. Or free to manage their own money (if they had any).

In the UK, women could not open a bank account in their own name, or apply for a business loan, or a mortgage, unless they had a male guarantor, until 1975.

Yes, you read that date right.

In the West, women could not vote until the late 19th or early 20th centuries. Cambridge University did not award degrees to women until 1943. Harvard Medical School did not admit women until 1945.

No woman could have done what Charles Darwin did and voyage round the world as an independent scientist.

A woman's world was tiny. It's hard to think big when your world is tiny.

Without a community of peers – interesting people talking about interesting things – it is hard to think at all.

To me, it's not astonishing that most women could not contribute to society – what's astonishing is how much women have contributed since we've been able to educate our minds, earn our own money, vote in elections and build independent lives.

How long is that? Not much more than a hundred years. In reality, equal pay and equal rights weren't enshrined in law in the West till the 1970s. And even when a law is in force, societal norms take time to change.

As a woman who is from a working-class background, I was aware, growing up, how little was expected of me in terms of achievement. It was assumed by my teachers that, like other girls, I too might go into teaching, or train as a nurse (not a doctor), or get a job to bide my time till marriage.

Ambition was for others.

It was not for the working class. It was not for working-class women.

This has nothing to do with genetics. Nothing to do with individual attributes or interests. Nothing to do with what's natural. It is about social circumstances. It is about socially engineered inequality.

The unscientific lie that all women are inferior to men, that most men are inferior to other men, that non-whites are inferior to whites is a tidy but simple-minded way to avoid any kind of social justice. These are not 'hard truths'. They are lies.

Outliers, like Ada Lovelace and George Boole, don't prove the theory of a few exceptional people who will break through anyway, showing that social mobility is possible if you just worked harder and had some talent (and, if you are female, maybe a sex change).

The talent-myth is a heartbreaking reminder of the wasted potential of so many lost and invisible others. Lost and invisible because of skin colour, or gender, or their place in the class system. People with fixed fates whose stories are not supposed to change. The few who do break through are there to prove that the system is right and fair. Whether the system is based on God or genes.

Genetic inheritance is real. No doubt about that. Organisms select and carry forward genetic material via reproduction. That's a true story. But is it the whole story? And is it the story of our lives?

A gene is a segment of DNA that provides a cell with detailed instructions on how to do its job. Few diseases are 100 per cent genetic. A tiny percentage, like Huntingdon's, are genetic, which means that if you have the gene, you have the disease. There is a breast cancer gene, which does increase your chances of getting cancer by about 50 per cent, but only 7 per cent of women with breast cancer carry that gene.

In 2003, when the Human Genome Project concluded the first stage of its work, there was a euphoric belief that here was the answer to everything. Humans were a code. The code could be read. Newspaper headlines told us this was the language of life.

More than twenty years later, when medical science hasn't found the magic genes that will explain everything, the newer discoveries of epigenetics suggest something very different.

It is our experiences, and our environment, acting on our genetic inheritance, that will determine how our genes will express themselves. Genes can be switched on and genes can be switched off.

Genes are stories that have been written. So far so true. When we look closer, we find something else. Gene *expression* is a story that goes on being written.

You are a work in progress.

Nature versus Nurture is simple – and simplistic. Really, we are talking about Nature with Nurture. It's not a binary.

The study of epigenetics has prompted us to think beyond gradual mutation and natural selection. Darwin was right – of course he was right – but the way with stories is that they are never the full story, or the only story. The Greek word 'epi' is the prefix English uses to denote 'on top of', 'among' or 'in addition to'. Epigenetics is the study of modifications to gene expression that happen all the time and *without* alteration to the genetic code itself.

What we know now is that life on the outside acts on life on the inside.

Genes answer to their environment.

This can seem even more fatalistic – for instance, stressed mother rats produce stressed pups. Is this yet another example of Blame Mum? No, we aren't blaming Mum. It's not her fault her environment is sub-optimal. And while her own experiences will adversely affect normal stress responses in her pups, that response can be unlearned. It's an epigenetic response, not a genetic blueprint.

There's a way out.

*

What starts as a bad beginning doesn't have to lead inexorably to a bad ending – or worse, an endless intergenerational Greek tragedy where no one can escape their fate.

One of the things I love about fiction is that we can – and do – escape our fate.

A word of caution here. This may not mean the characters in the story.

Often, they don't escape. We read with mounting horror, or frustration, as immoveable forces seem to determine an ending no one wants. Please bear in mind that when we read, our sense of bafflement, or injustice or compassion or anger, is the route by which we, the reader, might understand something that allows us to fight for change in the world, or to find the key that will unlock the seeming fixity of our own lives.

When *Madame Bovary* was first published in France in 1856, three years before Darwin's *On the Origin of Species*, there was an outcry against the appearance of a new form of 'insanity' in women who read that novel. Bovarysme was the name of the disease for every middle-class wife who rebelled against her circumstances.

Madame Bovary doesn't end well for Madame Bovary. For the women who read it, it was like a message in a bottle; they weren't crazy or weird or alone. Other women – nice, middle-class women – felt this way too. They felt trapped, depressed, they had dangerous affairs. And they felt this way and acted this way not because they had a disease, not because they were 'degenerate', not because they were born bad but because of the crushing personal consequences of their social and domestic situation.

*

Stories are there to change *what is* into *what if?*
What if I'm not crazy? What if I'm not trapped? What if things were different? Then what?

My mother knew nothing about genetics. Along with 'What's bred in the bone comes out in the marrow' she enjoyed 'The apple doesn't fall far from the tree.'

This got mangled into Eve eating the apple in the Garden of Eden and the rotten apple spoiling everything in the barrel. These illustrations were used to convey to me that I was born bad because my bio-ma was 'bad' (what kind of a woman puts her baby up for adoption?). On the other hand, if I was also so bad maybe she had done the right thing? I was never sure.

All my childhood and teenage behaviours were interpreted using various biological and hereditary fictions. And I accepted it. My only hope was to be saved.

When being saved by Jesus no longer worked for me intellectually, I tried to find lovers who would save me emotionally. Energetically, I worked to save others too. My baseline tale is disaster/rescue. Or, just as likely, rescue/disaster.

My parents maintained that they tried hard to rescue me. I believe them – even though I know now that they were really trying to rescue their marriage.

In any case, the lifebelt they threw me was too small. It felt like a straitjacket to me. I was argumentative and withdrawn. My mother declared she had been cheated. 'The Devil led us to the wrong crib.'

I have got a lot of things right in my life – found meaningful work and made good friends, but I can't manage close relationships. Intimacy makes me anxious. It's fight, flight, freeze. Or fawn.

I have heard this kind of childhood trauma described as 'the old present'. The bad stuff may be in the past, in that it is no longer an active part of the present, but what if the mind is stuck on repeat, telling itself the same old story – because it is the story it has learned by heart?

The failure of so many well-meaning interventions, whether on a personal level, or the societal level, is this: If we simply airlift a human from a terrible place to a better one, the terrible place comes along too, because it is already imprinted in the circuitry of self. To untangle and reset that terribleness is no small task. Your fate is not fixed, but there's going to be a lot of work to do. It's not just the new story that needs to be heard and accepted – the old story has to be understood for what it was, and why it was.

Can that old story be managed? Healed even?

I believe so.

I believe so, although I know I am far from fully healed up, and likely I never will be, but I do know where the damage is, and how it came about. There's no blame any more, but there is useful knowledge.

And there are, too, the liberating fictions that allowed me to alter the facts of my life. Without those stories I don't think I would be alive today.

Melodramatic? As Saul Bellow puts it: *More die of heartbreak.*

Hearts break when hope is gone.

No doctor can heal heartbreak. No medicine. No operation. There are two remedies though.

Love is one. If you are lucky. Imagination is the other. You don't need luck for that. That's lucky . . .

I used literature/language to develop and strengthen my mind – and that was important. I learned how to think. But thinking isn't enough.

Imagination is key. To see past the present, with its assumptions and constraints. To see round corners.

For me, it was reading. It was literature. But all art is there to develop our imaginative capacity.

That's crucial.

We can imagine other lives – including our own. More importantly, I think, we can imagine other outcomes.

What I realised on the street, all those years ago, was that I could read myself as a fiction as well as fact. The story could change.

WHAT HAPPENS NEXT?

The merchant in our first story has been home to put his affairs in order. He follows his temporary reprieve. A year passes. Another day comes. If no one can escape their fate, can anyone who is mortal escape time?

'No!' says the clock.

'Yes!' says the story.

The next part of our story opens Shahrazad's second night. She should be dead by now.

Here he comes. The merchant. He looks older. Only a year of clock-time. Lifetimes of regret. If only he had been somewhere else. If only he hadn't lobbed the date stone. If only the Ifrit had been out shopping.

Well, here he is. The oasis is just as he left it, palm trees swaying gently in the evening breeze. It's cool and beautiful. He's alone.

No. He's not alone. The scene is not exactly as he left it. Look closer. Who's that, leaning against a tree, drinking from a leather bottle?

It's an old man. The old man is leading a gazelle on a golden chain.

The two travellers greet each other in the customary way, offering food and drink to share.

The Old Man says: 'Take what you like. I am on a long journey.'

The Merchant says: 'Eat all you want. I am here to die.'

The Old Man looks confused. The Merchant tells him his tale.

Just then, at the moment of what is surely the whole story and its ending, the gentle breeze turns to a wild gust, and the wild gust whips into a wind, and the wind makes itself into a tornado that bends the trees and covers the travellers in sand. The gazelle has lain down.

Melodramatic as ever, it's the Ifrit coming to claim the merchant's life.

'Prepare to die!' says the Ifrit, unsheathing a scimitar.

'Spare me!' begs the Merchant

'Spare him in the name of Allah!' pleads the Old Man.

'Never!' yells the Ifrit. 'Kneel down, you dog, and be done with it!'

The Merchant kneels down. The Ifrit raises his blade.

In the second that beats between rise and fall, between life and death, the Old Man steps forward. He asks the Ifrit if he would like to hear a wondrous tale in exchange for one third of the merchant's blood?

(Author's note: In those days you could buy/bargain/own outright someone else's body parts including their fluids. I say 'those days' because in the USA at the moment there is a battle over who owns a woman's womb and its contents. Anyway, in our story, this bargain is a clever ruse because the old man will get a say in what happens to the merchant.)

There is a pause. The Ifrit has travelled a long way. The beheading will be over in a second. He's bored.

(Author's note: When Ifrits are not outraged, they are bored.)

All right. Why not? He agrees to wait a while and hear the wondrous tale, and if it is sufficiently wondrous, yes, he will share the Merchant's blood with the Old Man.

The Merchant pokes up his head from the sand. If this is the last thing he hears, it had better be good.

The Old Man says: 'Prepare to marvel at my words.'

But Shahryar will have to wait because it's morning again.

START AGAIN

Shahrazad's first tale, like her own situation, is the story of someone who doesn't deserve their fate. Not a hero, no one special, an ordinary person in the wrong place at the wrong time. Life is unfair, unreasonable, seemingly random. The story hasn't started well.

Fortunately, a story started doesn't stop at once. Yet that's what happens to many millions of people in the world. Their story is stopped as soon as it has begun. Or before it has a chance to develop. Human beings need a chance to develop. Our personal stories are not micro-fictions.

Our stories are not one story either. The *Nights* shies away from telling the whole thing in one go – beginning, middle, end. Instead, *Nights* narratives break off, break out, flow wilfully into other tales. What we hear, as we go in and out of the lives of others, comes to have a bearing on the earlier adventures, no matter how distant. The message here is that all of life is connected by an endless web of stories, moving and changing. That brings hope.

The way into each story is fixed. You could say, genetically fixed. There's a situation. *What is.*

The way through, and eventually the way out of, the

story, is a branching, multiplying, often contradictory series of *what ifs?*

Nights stories aren't the Eastern version of the Western trope of the Hero. You know the one – character is destiny, life is a series of battles to be won, there's a prize at the end, and everyone else depends on the saviour that is you.

In *Nights*, nothing is so self-aggrandising.

Yes, there are tough guys and adventurers, chancers and conmen, innocents and double-crossers, comedy figures, paupers who gain palaces and princesses, and mean little schemers who get nothing. But these aren't morality tales in the sense of who is deserving and who is undeserving. No Survival of the Fittest. No action-man to save the world.

Plus, and this matters, everyone who does get a good outcome, relies on a big dollop of luck.

The *Nights* does though, like any drama, thriller, or action-man story, from the East or the West, get started when things are in a state of upheaval. This is just the same with European fairy tales too. The King is useless, the Queen is plotting, there's a dragon, there's a famine, there's a thoughtless entitled idiot who's going to lose his daughter to a goblin . . . and so on.

The *Nights* then follows a very different route.

The solution to these stories is always outside of what might be expected to happen. As events unfold, the story disrupts its own algorithm. The series of steps does not lead where it should.

Your beginning in life – poor fisherman/King/simple girl – will not be the major force propelling the outcome.

Good qualities – courage, kindness, patience – will help you out, and so do personal attributes like quick wits, or strength, or skill. Paranoia, or nastiness, or cowardice will get in the way.

What matters most, though, are chance encounters with others.

I have to write that again. In caps. It matters.
ENCOUNTERS WITH OTHERS.

These 'others' might be human or supernatural beings. It makes no difference. These encounters will alter the regular flow of the narrative. In a Hero narrative – yes, there are other people – foes, lovers, buddies, family – but the Hero remains a Lone Star figure. He's the One. Like Neo in the Matrix movies, like Luke Skywalker in Star Wars. Like James Bond. Sherlock Holmes. Doctor Who. Jack Reacher. Any Mission Impossible movie. The outcome depends on our Hero.

It usually is a Him.

The *Nights* is not about heroes. Who you meet, how you meet them, whether they decide to help or to hinder, to notice, to ignore, whether you decide to engage or walk on by, makes all the difference to the outcome.

Shahrazad herself, a hero if ever there was one, is not a lone star. She depends on every story she tells, and every story she tells exposes the listener/reader to the importance of interventions by others.

In contrast, Shahryar vaunts himself as a Dark Anti-Hero, the one avenging all men. He's the power who decides life and death.

Shahrazad sets out to show him, and us, that life is not a series of solos. It's an ensemble. Life is a web. Stories birth new stories. Not one grand story. Not one of a handful of basic plots – where you, the hero, will overcome the danger thanks to your own special powers.

Encounters affect outcomes because . . .

Nobody in the *Nights* says, 'This is none of my business.'

SHAPE-SHIFTING
FOR BEGINNERS

The Old Man is sitting cross-legged, his back against a palm tree. The Ifrit sits cross-legged too, floating a little above the sand, to show his superiority. The Merchant lies on his back looking at the first star.

Now begin.

The gazelle you see before you, so tame and pretty, is my wife. We were married for thirty years but she bore me no child. Naturally, I took another wife, as Allah allows, and had a child by her, a son as beautiful as the moon.

When my boy was fifteen, I had to travel some distance and was gone for some time. While I was away, my first wife determined to take her revenge. She had studied the magic arts in her youth, and without further ado, she turned the mother of my son into a fat cow. Next, she turned my son into a calf.

When I returned home, my wife told me that my son had run away after his mother had died.

For many months I mourned.

There came a day when I needed a beast for the feast. My herdsman brought me a fine fat cow, but as soon as I drew my knife, the cow roared and kicked, so much so that I was ready to spare her. I would have spared her, but my wife intervened, calling me a fool. She threatened me and belittled me. I steeled my resolve. Go on! Go on! Yet still I could not kill the cow. I ordered the herdsman to slaughter her for me. As he slit her throat I looked into her eyes. I could swear she was speaking to me.

My wife went indoors laughing.

It was strange. Do you hear me? Strange. Once dead, the fine fat cow was nothing but skin and bone. Inside the hide, there was nothing. No meat, no flesh.

I regretted listening to my wife because now I would need to slaughter a second beast. This time a much smaller calf was brought to me. As the calf was led in on the rope, he lay down in the dust, rolling and kicking and pleading with his eyes. My wife returned to the door, wiping her hands on her apron.

'You coward! You fool! Do your job!'

To silence her voice, I tucked up my clothes and lifted the blade above the trembling calf.

At this, the sun rises, and Shahrazad breaks off the story.

When we look closely at this story, we notice a common theme in the *Nights*: a questioning theme. Who is to blame?

The old man is not to blame for his situation. He had no knowledge of his wife's deceit.

That is certainly true. Yet, if we were sitting round the fire hearing this story, we might say to one another – well, perhaps he isn't to blame, but should he take some responsibility?

A man finding himself a new wife was not a legal or cultural problem, as this was normal practice. Islam permits polygamy for men.

So yes, indeed, in the eyes of the law the man is blameless here.

But what happens if we look at the situation from the point of view of his original wife?

It can't have been fun, aged forty-five or so, to see a young pregnant slip of a girl prancing about with the family's son and heir. Very likely Mrs Wife thought of her replacement as a cow. And that's what she becomes. There are plenty of times when we'd like to be able turn someone into a cow, or a rat, or a pig, or a snake. It seems to suit them.

Shape-shifting in stories is never random. The human turned into an animal has an affinity with the creature whose shape they must bear. Maybe little Miss Lovely *was* a bit of a cow . . .

We can understand the wife's point of view. She is powerless in her husband's decision-making. She too finds herself in a mess not of her own making. Wifely revenge on younger, prettier rivals is nothing new. Not because women are petty and mean, but because when women lack agency over their own lives, and when women are treated as worn-out goods to be replaced, it doesn't bring out the best in us.

This wife, though, has hatred in her heart. She doesn't settle for her triumph. She wants the death penalty.

Worse yet, she plots for her husband to be the executioner.

As the story breaks off here, the listener knows that what has brought us to the place is action in the past. What's at stake now is the future. What's in the balance is justice. The boy-calf *really* isn't to blame for any of this. He's not a hero, or a villain. He's an ordinary person caught in a dire situation. He's not a wild animal, he's a piece of domestic livestock, like his dead mother. Did Mrs Wife realise that without the aid of magic power, women and children are all pieces of domestic livestock? Their lives at the mercy of others.

Shahrazad knows this. Hundreds of blameless young women have already been murdered by Shahryar, just because he can.
Now what?

In the *Nights*, as in the Arthurian legends, as in so many fairy and folk tales, women gain magical power to offset their lack of social and political power. This trope carries right through to the witch frenzy of the 16th and 17th centuries in Britain, mainland Europe, and the early American settlements. It is intimately connected to male fear of autonomous female sexuality. That's how the *Nights* starts.

The absolute power a woman can wield over a man is always described as sexual power. The ultimate thrall. It is experienced as enchantment. Bewitchment. A man loses his senses. He loses his mind. No longer in charge of himself, his lover controls him. He's a lapdog.
Or worse.
In the *Odyssey*, the enchantress Circe is known for transforming men into beasts – and when Odysseus's sailors arrive on her island, scoff her food and behave like louts, she turns them into pigs.
Remember: the shape-shift is never random – not just any old animal form – it's specific.
Odysseus's men are soldiers and sailors. Men who like to get their heads in the trough. Terrible table manners.
Circe deals with them accordingly. Her punishment is a

like-for-like comment on their grunting, belching, farting, drunken behaviour. *And get your groping trotters off my girls*, says Circe.

Reappearing the sailors as pigs is a good joke. A punishment on behalf of all the women the men have treated swinishly along the way.

Men in war, then and now, rape women and children as an accepted part of the spoils of war. Spoils is a noun, but as a verb what is spoiled? The lives of the women and girls, certainly. Also, the loving, protective, *human* nature of the men. On the surface of the situation, it looks as though men can just walk away from their crimes, but they leave behind the most important thing they possess: their humanity.

But while men shape-shift *themselves* into a creature that is debased, a woman who is treated as an object, as a prize, as a piece of flesh, as a spoil, has been shape-shifted against her will.

Women are routinely shape-shifted against their will.

Social pressure to look a certain way, to dress a certain way, can easily become a permanent shape-shift. A woman has feet flat on the ground – just as a man does. Why then is it normal/expected for her to wear shoes that stand her on tiptoes? She's not Barbie.

A woman has hair all over her body, just as a man does, though generally less of it. Why then must a woman's hair sit on her head, but nowhere else? Why is a woman who prefers not to wear make-up seen as making a statement (women are not encouraged to make statements) or is she just not making an effort? Is she only natural in disguise?

Men are raised to feel comfortable in their bodies, not because Nature made the male body a more comfortable place to be, but because Nurture primes women to get used to a lifetime of discomfort. The clothes that don't keep her warm, the shoes she can't walk in – does my bum look big in this?

What a woman wears, and how a woman looks, is how a woman will be judged – by men, certainly, but by other women too, whose accepting allegiance to the asymmetrical norms of patriarchy is part of the teamwork that keeps the illusion real.

As we read the *Nights*, those questions keep coming in – is this real? Is this an illusion? The right answer can save your life.

In the *Nights*, anyone with magic power can alter their size – smaller than small, bigger than big – genies that puff up to 300 feet tall can pack into jam jars.

In our world, there are millions of women who have studied the dark arts of shrinkage.

We learn how to disappear as much of ourselves as seems surplus to requirements.

But whose requirements?

How many times have you seen the guy with the shirt gaping over his gut, tucking into his pasta and red wine, while his gorgeous girlfriend eats a salad? With water.

It used to be that how you looked and how you lived was only of interest to a small circle – your home, your hometown, your friends. And if men have always had the opportunity to get away, when social pressure at home proved too much – well, women won that opportunity too, in the 20th century. We got jobs, made money – we were gaining independence.

What happened? Suddenly, we're all living in the Hotel California. The model for social media. Check out any time you like, but you can never leave.

Social pressure can be avoided. Social media is unavoidable.

Social media doesn't just follow you wherever you go, keeping its watchful eye on you like a private investigator. Social media gets right inside us because we are inside it.

Literally living inside it. Every bit of the self that is data is tracked. A carapace hardens around us made up of this data. There is no escape. You can run but you can't hide, and if you do plan to run, an ad will pop up on your phone for a pair of air-soled Nikes.

Social media 'playfully' give us the tools to alter our appearance in posts. To go further than that, and offer ourselves to the world as someone we are not. A shape-shift that satisfies others, or, in the age-old way, deliberately sets out to deceive others.

Social media dresses itself up as empowerment for all. The *Nights* teaches us to look past the outward show . . . is this really what it seems? This person? This palace?

Look again. Look behind the seductions. Strip it bare. It's ugly. It's coercive control.

What did Simone de Beauvoir say in *The Second Sex* (1949)?

> *On ne naît pas femme: on le devient.*
> *One is not born but rather becomes a woman.*

This is not a natural becoming. It's not the Quest. It's not the Hero's Journey. It's how to behave so that the Hero can have his own journey. Women are discouraged from discovering their authentic self. To be self-possessed (note the verb with its magical connotations) makes it impossible to be possessed by others.

The shape-shifts in the *Nights* are not fantasy. They are psychological realities. How do you appear to others? How do you appear to yourself? Is it really you?

But there is another kind of shape-shifting. It's not done to you – it's done by you.

It happens often in the *Nights*. In these tales, sorcerers, shamans, witches, messengers of the gods, the gods themselves can alter their external form.

For non-biological beings, shape-shifting is a manifestation of their unbounded condition. They are not fixed as humans are. Their appearance can change at will. Their form is a matter of choice.

Humans feel bewilderment and disbelief that we are confined to our bodies. Bodies that age and die. Religion might have been invented to convince us that this depressing fact of life is a fiction. The body can't contain us. Religion regards our physical form as approximate and temporary – and so does magic.

In the modern world, video games and virtual reality zones allow body-bound humans to play at being someone or something else. Choose an avatar. Don't like it? Choose another one.

If the metaverse develops beyond its current, clunky, low-grade attempt at monetising desire, we might see the creation of a meaningful space where anyone can try out being anything, with a way to return, and without fear or judgement. You could have a second life, not as a bit of silly escapism, but as an expression of the you that is not met, or served, in the usual world.

Yes, it might turn into an abusive fascist state, like so much of social media, but it doesn't have to be that way.

And isn't it the case that always, and forever, humans have longed to be done with fixity? Yes, because fixity includes death – this is the one and only you, and it will pass away. But also, more philosophically, because being caught in this body doesn't feel like the truth. It feels damn well wrong.

To be or not to be may not always be the question. To be more may be the answer.

Ovid's *Metamorphoses* begins like this:

> *In nova fert animus mutatas dicere formas /*
> *Corpora.*

Using the poet Ted Hughes' inspired translation, this reads:

> *Now I am ready to tell how bodies are changed / Into different bodies.*

The body should not be identified with the self in a permanent way.

I realise this opens me up to a charge of Cartesian

dualism – the old-fashioned Mind–Body split – yet I do not accept that the body is the sum of the self. Not least because the body is a thing in process.

Your body, even your brain, is in a state of constant change. Every day, cells are replaced. Skin and gut within weeks. Your skeleton over ten years. Sure, you still look like 'you', just older. But the 'you' that is 'you' is not a solid. The process is a pattern of information. The problem is that we have little control over this process/pattern – and as yet, no capacity to make the kinds of changes that magic used to be so good at. Fed up with being fat and forty? Let's change it. Try flying over the city as an eagle tonight.

At present, 'walk on air against your better judgement', as Seamus Heaney put it, is what we can do imaginatively, and it can change everything. But we can't do it physically, though we love every story and cartoon that shows us someone who can.

So many stories. Today I am a greyhound. Tomorrow I am a beautiful girl. Today I have no corporeal presence. Tomorrow I am by your side.

This is feasible only in fairy tale or sci-fi or poetry, but look to that wisdom. What we imagine, we invent.

Wonder-tales, like the *Nights*, contain truths that may be read as symbolic or psychological, and that's valuable enough, but as we accelerate forward into a world driven by AI, those truths look like they might take shape in the reality of our lives. Maybe we won't be confined by the body after all. How does that feel?

Wonderful? Frightening?

I think we will be fine with that long overdue change of

status. We have been rehearsing it for thousands of years in the stories we tell.

Fictions are not make-believe. We have come to understand this better through the medium of sci-fi, as so much of what begins as a futuristic fantasy becomes an ordinary part of the world we know.

Fiction is much more than social-realist cut-outs of contemporary life. More than representation. Fiction declares and debates inner realities that gradually press forward into our outer circumstances. We catch up with our dreams.

One thing we know for sure is that each of us is more than what lies on the surface.

Our multiple, mobile, many-selves – the multiplicity we get in touch with whenever we sit quietly and ask who we really are, when we look at a photo and wonder 'is that me?', when we catch ourselves in a mirror and see someone else – these fleeting discomforts point to another ancient shape-shifting trope, and there are plenty of examples in the *Nights*.

True form.

There are so many stories where, if you fight for long enough, or hold on for long enough, the entity you are grappling with will toggle through its options, at speed, and often fiercely, only to reveal itself, finally, as it actually is. Everyone knows about Princess Fiona in *Shrek*: 'By night one way, by day another . . .' until love sets her free.

It's the same for frogs who should be princes and beasts who should be human.

Changelings are said to have a true form – if you can find it.

*

'Form' denotes the physical shape or configuration of something.

How it presents to others.

For many, a false self is the only form of self that feels safe to show. The only acceptable self. We all have to play a part sometimes. We all need a work front and a meeting new people front, perhaps a public speaking front, all the helpful guises, and disguises, that get us through the day. We talk about finding someone with whom we can be ourselves.

But that's just it – is it self or selves? Our true form may not be one thing at all.

When I was growing up, being gay and lesbian felt like simultaneously hiding a true self and finding a true self. It was really me, but it was not a me that was acceptable to my family or to my church. More upsetting is the fact that when we are young, we need time and space and acceptance to explore our different, sometimes contradictory, selves. I felt that my process of *becoming* was forced too soon into a statement of *being*.

I don't mean I would likely have changed my mind and married the vicar, if I hadn't been pushed to define my sexuality, and my self for the sake of others. Rather, it took me much longer than it need have done to understand my sexuality as a *response* – as fluid and unfixed as the rest of me. I don't experience my sexuality as a given – like my height. For me, it doesn't feel like I was born this way. It was, and is, a series of choices, and earlier in my life, unconscious choices. Yet the labels were applied faster than my understanding could rip them off.

The literalness of labels is depressing. I wanted an imaginative way to discover how to be me. *Who* to be me? Desiring other girls was part of that. It wasn't a pathology. It wasn't genetic. It wasn't a lifestyle choice. It was part of my evolution.

For now, at least in most of Europe and north America, queerness is not the hideaway state it used to be. Folks can live their lives as gay or straight or somewhere in between. Many younger people identify as non-binary. The trans movement has forced us all to think more deeply, and with more difficulty, about the relationship between biological sex and gender expression.

Not *What is*. *What if?*

Many trans folks talk about finding their true form via hormone therapy and surgery, so that what they see in the mirror, and how others see them, aligns with how they recognise themselves.

I understand this. It's good and it's right and should be celebrated. The anger that is rife just now between trans women (it doesn't seem to be trans men) and those women who are labelled as exclusionary feminists, must be resolved. At the core of the problem, I think, maybe, is that the long history of being born a woman is a history of being told by men *what is*. Feminism challenged and rewrote that dismal history by asking *what if?*

What if none of the things we had been told about ourselves has any basis in reality? What if it's all a grand fiction?

And so, it is difficult to hear some trans women, born and raised as male in a world that still privileges maleness, explain to women born into the battle for every inch of personal space, private space, safe space, equal space, that we have no right to that exclusive space. For women whose history is one of silence – no debate about that – it is all too familiar to hear our voices shouted down and our lived experience ignored.

And then I think about trans women who have been through so much to find their identity – their authenticity – and they too are not being heard. It feels like rejection. Not a real woman. Well, lesbians are used to that kind of insult. Women who aren't behaving quite as a man would like are used to it too. And it's not a rejection I want anyone to feel.

There has to be a way through this stand-off. A way to find a story that is not based on rejection and recrimination. We know how those stories end. No one wins.

Biological essentialism – *this is a woman, that is a man* – has never been a story for everyone. For millions, it's been a prison, for millions more, it's limited but comforting. In a bewildering world, it can look like a shelter. A certainty. There's a backlash against gender non-conformity now, after some decades of tolerance and inclusivity. Extremists like Andrew Tate preach the biological inferiority of women. So does the Taliban. Right-wing apologists for men behaving badly call it 'nature'. Men are born this way.

To be Trans is to be part of the spectrum of Being. Wider and freer than any of those too-small binaries.

We will shortly be interacting on a daily basis, an enmeshed basis, with smart systems – embodied (robots) and not, that have no biology and no gender.

The non-binary world is already here.

The non-binary world is the future.

At present we give AI a gender. Usually female if it's 'helpful' AI.

To me that's boring and backward. We are in the process of developing a fluid, likely intelligent system, that is definitely not subject to our biological grid, and that need not be interpreted, sold, or marketed using our limited ideas around gender.

Perhaps this will become clearer as we merge with AI systems – allowing us to connect directly to the AI world, probably via a BCI (brain-computer interface) chip in our brains.

This isn't far-fetched. BCI implants are already able to help patients with physical and neurological traumas to connect directly to their laptop – just by thinking their thoughts.

Taking it further – Larry Page at Google has been explicit about the function of BCI chips – you will no longer need to connect to a device . . . you will be the device. It will be like having your own personal genie. Ask a question and the answer is already there.

By 2030, engineer and futurologist Ray Kurzweil predicts, nanobots will flood our bodily biological systems to check our vital health signals – blood pressure, blood sugar, heart rate, respiration and so on – and to repair the damage of ageing at a cellular level. This is wonderful news, if it comes true on a practical level, but symbolically, it's a huge leap. This is when the Kingdom of the Body loses its hard boundaries – just as it does in shape-shifting.

The separations between self and other, male and female, straight and gay – the handy definitions we've lived by – are on their way out. AI in its pure form has no skin colour, no biological sex, no gender.

Think about that . . .

*

Later on, when perhaps we may be able to upload consciousness, then biological sex and gender become irrelevant.

This isn't the end of the human – unless you think being human begins and ends with biology.

Reading *The Arabian Nights*, we find that biology isn't anyone's sum total – things happen along the way.

Being human in the *Nights* can mean appearing in other shapes and other forms.

Being human in the *Nights* means accepting different life forms who don't share your biology – but whose special powers you can sometimes share – like travelling instantly across space. Teleporting.

Being human in the *Nights* is to accept that swallowing the right potion can reverse ageing or give you clairvoyant powers. Your biology is never the final word.

We are more than we seem to be.

The multiplicity inside us isn't a series of contradictions. The only problem is if we get stuck in a shape that isn't ours. When the persona hardens around the person. When the mask has fused with our face. When acting like a brute turns us into a brute. When not being able to settle means we can only fly away. When I become your faithful dog, your beast of burden, your golden goose, your mermaid, because I want intimacy but not sex. When I live my life like a fish out of water.

Here I am. Your gazelle on a chain.

Shahrazad said to the Sultan:

King of the World, what follows is more marvellous yet.

I'M TELLING
YOU STORIES.
TRUST ME.

Unable to bring himself to kill the calf, the old man turned away. His wife spat on the ground, cursing his hesitation. The herdsman, with nothing left to do, and seeing it was too late in the day to return the calf to the herd, led the calf on a rope to his own home.

As the herdsman neared his house, his daughter ran out, laughing and crying at the same time, asking him why he thought so little of her that he would bring a strange man into her presence?

The herdsman was bewildered. He respected his daughter. What strange man?

His daughter pointed to the calf. At this, the calf laid down.

Now, the daughter had learned early in life that skill in magic arts was essential for a woman. She had studied in secret with a sorceress from the village.

The herdsman's daughter explained to her father that the calf was under an enchantment. This was not his true form. In reality, the calf was the long-lost son.

What could the herdsman do but wait out the time until morning?

As soon as it was light, he rushed to his master. The old man was outside, lighting a fire, watching the morning sun begin.

His heart was heavy. He warmed his hands at the fire and his eyes at the rising sun.

The herdsman delivered the astonishing news.

Together, they hurried through the village to where the daughter and the calf waited patiently.

Is this a true story?

Yes! It is a true story.

Now what?

The girl explained that she could return the young man to his true form. Rejoice! Rejoice! But there is a condition.

Oh?

The fathers must agree to a wedding. Daughter and Calf-Boy.

The old man is laughing with joy. 'Is that all? The answer is Yes! Oh, and take as many of my cattle as you can count.'

This is going well . . .

'Ah!' says the girl. 'Prepare to be astonished.'

She mixes secret herbs with water. The calf lies at her feet. The men watch in silence.

'Ah!' says the girl. 'If calf you be, calf remain. If man you be, as man return.'

She sprinkles the calf with the dark-coloured infused water. The calf blinks and licks the drops from his cheeks. He stumbles to stand. Not four legs now, only two, and there before them is a fine young man, with deep black eyes and long eyelashes, weeping tears of joy.

For an hour, at least, everyone talks, and everyone listens, and everyone does this all at once.

'Ah!' says the girl. 'This celebration is all well and good, but unless I curb your wife's instinct for harm, more harm will be done.'

'Kill her!' says the old man.

'Kill her!' says the herdsman.

'Kill her!' says the son.

But no. The new daughter-in-law chooses a different punishment. Like for like. Shape-shift for shape-shift.

His wife will become . . . What? A rat? A hyena? A snake? A vulture?

No. No.

A gazelle.

Huh?

Look closer.

The Arabic word for gazelle is ghazaal.

There's an Arabic branch of love poetry called ghazal, whose poems end in loss, separation, or sadness. This theme of loss ties in with another meaning of ghazaal – not just a deer or an antelope, but specifically, the painful wail of a wounded deer.

Mrs Wife, trained in magic arts, like her unexpected new daughter-in-law, will know exactly how her punishment fits her crimes.

Mrs Wife has lost. Her wounded wail is all that remains.

If we freeze-frame the story here, if we stand back and look again, what do we notice?

Here are three men – two fathers and a young man – whose futures lie in the hands of a young woman.

This is a reversal of the typical situation where men hold

the power. For a while, another woman, Mrs Wife, had taken control of the domestic drama – but she did it secretly and dishonestly. Our young woman is obvious and honest. No games. She is telling the truth to everyone – and that is why she can also control the vengeful lying wife.

The power balance has shifted because here is someone who can see into the life of things. Someone who can see beneath the surface.

What is real. What is an illusion.

This young woman alone will decide how the story continues.

She is an avatar for Shahrazad herself.

People ask me, what is the point of reading literature?

By literature I mean those works of the imagination that are more than page-turners to pass the time and be tossed away. Once read and twice forgotten.

Literature allows complexity, but complexity doesn't mean obscurity. Literature doesn't mean boring. What we are hoping for – well, what I am hoping for – is a piece of work with the power to captivate us on many levels.

Yes, we want the story. Yes, we want a relationship with the characters. Yes, we want to enter this new – maybe strange – world. And then we want something to happen, by which I mean something to happen to *us.*

This new, maybe strange, world will pose questions, will prompt memories, will cause us to reflect on our own world. And matters of the heart. We always end up there.

Literature is an invention. But it's an invention that asks us to distinguish between reality and illusion.

The easy answers on the surface are often illusions. They don't go deep enough. The rules we live by are provisional and changing – things will never 'always be this way'. Things have never 'always been done this way'.

Shall we have a quick look at a classic text lots of people know – or think they know? Charlotte Brontë's *Jane Eyre*.

Here's a young woman, initially without friends or family or money – a dire situation for a young woman in the 19th century. Jane's answer to this misfortune is to meet every fresh challenge with a clear eye and a sound heart. Jane's superpower is the ability to discern what is false and what is true.

In the age of the gilded hypocrite, and at a time when a woman's opinion counted for little, this is quite a superpower.

Jane rejects marriage with the self-satisfied church minister, St John Rivers, because she doesn't love him. She sees through his liverish narcissism and recoils from his bloodless heart.

She refuses to live with the already married Mr Rochester as his mistress, not because she is a prude, but because she won't allow him the easy way out – something a man of his wealth and position takes for granted. She loves him deeply, but she values herself more deeply.

She doesn't want the second-rate option. This penniless young woman knows she is worth more than either man in her life is offering.

Later, of course, Jane *is* able to marry Mr Rochester. There is such a thing as a happy ending.

It's a story that has been diluted and cheapened by

romance novels the world over, but in the original, *Jane Eyre* is a difficult book to read. If we meet the novel on its own terms, it makes us uneasy. The obvious routes are blocked at every turn. To read *Jane Eyre*, as it asks to be read, is to question our own assumptions about what is the right response.

And for those who don't believe in metaphysical possibilities, the moment that Jane hears Mr Rochester calling to her across space-time, and she answers him, and rushes to Thornfield Hall, to find it burned down and himself blinded, well, this is a rebuke to literalness as powerful as anything in the magical-minded *Nights*.

Our common plane of existence is not the only plane of existence. Not everything that happens here has an answer here. We often need to go inside, to a spiritual or psychological plane. I was brought up religious, as you know, so I still look beyond, or through, what is only present in the here and now. That's the way I see life – all I can do is to be aware of it. My bias. Bias though, just means an inclination towards. What's yours?

Whatever your own personal bias might be, when you take a reading of life, you know as well as I do that even if our material needs are met, we realise, sometimes with dismay, that none of our big questions have been met at all. *Who am I? What am I? What am I doing here? Why is my heart broken?*

Make your own list.

The failure of this world is that so many people live in scarcity and lack. Maybe they are holding down two jobs, maybe not finding work at all. Many fear for their lives every day. There are millions of humans whose basic survival shuts them out of the breathing space to reflect on bigger questions, except perhaps via a religious creed that answers the questions for them. This can bring comfort and strength – but the work is left undone.

The big questions – if we are lucky enough to get to ask them – cannot be answered by anyone or anything, other than ourselves.

Not Jesus, not Allah, not the Buddha, not your guru, not your self-help books, not your family or even your partner. I am not advocating splendid isolation – far from it – the glory of human society is that we're not alone; we talk, we listen, we read, we learn from one another. Encounters affect outcomes. The great religions of the world, and the philosophers, and the thinkers, writers, who have gone before us, are all there to guide and to help. Our trusted loved ones are there to help.

Ultimately though, each must answer for herself. The same question will not be answered by you in the same way as it will be answered by me.

This is why literature is so valuable. Reading deeply is not time wasted. Reading is time set apart to get closer to ourselves. Alienation is the modern disease. Where do we belong? Where should our loyalties lie? This is really a deeper question about who we are. Belonging to yourself only happens when there is a way to dwell on – or do I mean dwell in? – the bigger questions.

And it's never over. Not till we die. And maybe not even then.

Who knows?

*

Karl Marx, bane of capitalism, not that his detractors seem to read him, believed that socialism should provide for man's animal needs – food, shelter, safety, a healthy environment, freedom from want – so that man could provide for his human needs. Curiosity, learning, study, invention, the arts, music, all the weird things that distinguish us from the animals. Through those things, we face the big existential questions. My purpose on this earth. *Who am I? What am I?*

Humans cannot live without meaning.

So no, your TikTok videos won't bring you meaning, neither will social media's weapons of mass distraction, that shrink the human mind to its smallest scope. Needing the next dopamine hit from the outside every few minutes is a miserable way to live. It's a strategy of discontent, and it makes it harder to settle down with a text that asks for our complete attention. Complete attention on the book might be a bit scary – because the next thing that happens is that you start to pay attention to your own inner life: Have you got one?

It's a good question. The poet Ted Hughes believed that we all have a soul, but that mostly, the soul is asleep. It doesn't need to bother to wake up to check the news, or to go shopping, or to sit in the office every day.

Hughes thought that it was the job of poetry to awaken the soul.

Poetry has more chance of escaping the mundane plane of existence than prose does because the chief property of poetry is language that goes beyond utility.

Such language prompts reverie and image-making. We are not caught only in what is going on – what happens next, a life of action – we are freed into a more creative, less goal-oriented, less anxious mental mode.

Utility is *the this and that* of our daily lives, the hamster-wheel of what another poet, William Wordsworth, called 'getting and spending'. Once our minds move past the utility level, the Soul rouses herself, and says: *This is worth getting up for.*

Now, I know that the search for something beyond utility leads many people to get lost in serial fantasy and/or video games, or to spend all their time online. It's a desperate cry for what the mundane world just can't offer – especially for those billions who now must live in impoverished/polluted environments, where nature can't do her work of both calming and stimulating us.

For me, the remedy many of us seek – knowingly or not – has to go deeper than escapism. Escape and escapism are not the same thing. Escapism is brief relief from what is intolerable. Escape is real.

In true *Nights* fashion, I will go on (another) detour here to tell you about the word ESCAPE.

The prefix e- or ex- is Latin for 'out of'. *Cappa* is Latin for a cloak with a hood – it started off as a female garment, but its meaning widened. So, when you escape, you are leaving your outer garment behind. This could involve a loss, but it's necessary.

When we escape the clutches of too much boring, draining, pointless life, we might have to leave something behind – but it's only an outer garment – and perhaps we take it off and hang it up, so we can slip away unnoticed.

There are plenty of reasons to slip away unnoticed.

Escapism – a very different word – doesn't appear in the English language until the early 1930s. Its usual use is negative – as a distraction from the rigours of real life – though fantasy writer Terry Pratchett tried to reclaim it, I suppose to defend his own work, not that his brilliant work needs defending.

If you are living inside *Discworld*, and that experience better equips you to live inside the real world, I wouldn't call it escapism. The problem with escapism is two-fold: distracting activities that make us more passive/compliant/accepting of the sub-optimal conditions of the real world. The situation in *The Hunger Games*, for instance, where the yearly gladiatorial torture-show of the Games is there to make the daily totalitarian dystopia bearable and accepted.

The other problem with escapism is that it is short-lived and ineffective. It's a drug from the outside that delivers nothing of substance and keeps us wanting more. I don't need to give you examples of how ruthlessly social media exploits this need in us. We are looking for escape. Social media substitutes escapism.

Don't get me wrong – you have a bad day and your friends say, 'forget it and come out for a drink'. That helps. It helps because you have friends, and because the light relief gives your mind a chance to calm down. Maybe you go to a sports event, maybe you go dancing or bowling. These activities are good fun and therapeutic. They 'take your mind off it'.

When I am not coping well, I work in the garden, or I take a walk alone. I look away from whatever it is that is distressing me, so that I can look again better, later.

Often, things bothering us can soon be mended. We're right to seek a little light relief to get things in perspective.

The big things though, well, a little light relief won't drive them away – they will still be there in the morning.

There is a huge difference between what we might call an existential crisis, and the regular ups and downs of life, or what Freud called 'ordinary unhappiness'.

When we are hitting the big questions, no amount of comfort, no amount of distraction, will help.

The reason I am an evangelist for literature is that steady, regular, engagement with deep thought, with lit-up language, with vivid worlds, encourages us to go *inwards, not outwards.*

Inwards is where we discover and create resources that belong to us.

Resources that are intrinsic not external.

I have a private library inside me that I can visit anytime. This is because I have stocked it over many years. In there are stories, characters, lines, words, ideas, comfort, challenge, memories, and even if I never saw a book again, no one can take away what I have.

They can't find it. It's not outside. It is inside.

This strategy of building a library on the inside started because my mother, Mrs Winterson, did try to take my books away.

In our religious house, books were secular, and not

allowed, unless they were anodyne, like her weekly diet of low-grade murder mysteries from the public library. I had to go and fetch the murder mysteries, so I soon discovered that real books existed.

English Literature in Prose A–Z was a magnificent wall of books set within the dignity and beauty of a Carnegie library – libraries built around the world with funds provided by the Scottish-American industrialist, Andrew Carnegie.

Provided for working-class folks, like me.

In the library, I found what I was looking for.

Mrs Winterson's rationale for No Books was simple: *The trouble with a book is that you never know what's in it till it's too late.*

She understood the power of literature.

These forbidden, powerful objects gained a magnetic fascination for me. I read them in the public library, while I was supposed to be choosing and collecting the murder mysteries, and I started to buy novels with money I earned after school at my job on the market stall.

If you want to know more about this time in my life, I have written about it in a memoir *Why Be Happy When You Could Be Normal?*

Books showed me that other worlds were possible. Other ways of thinking. Other ways of being. I was not just a poor child in a working-class town. A kid with limited options. I was Huck Finn, Heathcliff, Moomintroll, David Copperfield, Scout Finch, and while I was definitely not Emma Woodhouse or Dorothea Brook, I saw in those women the difficulty of being a woman – difficulty that had nothing to do with talent or intelligence and all to do with gender. The sclerotic narrowness of the prescribed female condition.

Remember *Madame Bovary*? And what a shock that book was to middle-class women who realised they weren't sick in the head or homewreckers.

I realised from my reading that many women are so trapped in the condition of being a woman that they have no opportunity to confront the bigger questions of life. *Who am I? What am I? What do I want?* And when they do so, the cost is high.

You might say, well, with all these books you talk about, why can't I just watch the movie? Movies are the modern world. Books are Before.

I love movies, though I don't often love movie adaptations of classics because too much is lost and too much is simplified.

Language is always a casualty.

Language itself, the words on the page – and the concentration of mind needed to read – widens and deepens our own mental capacity. And crucially, there is no one else interpreting the experience for us – no director, no scriptwriter, no actors. It's pure and direct. Your mind and the mind of the writer. It's a private conversation. An intimacy not found elsewhere.

I am a fan of audiobooks, but even there, we're likely to focus on story and miss much of what the language can offer – unless our minds are already trained to 'hear' language as language and not just as content delivery.

Sometimes, when you are reading, a sentence will knock you out – force you to pause – you will look up, think about what just overtook your whole self. Maybe you will underline it. Maybe you will always remember that line.

Reading is not linear in the way that audiobooks and movies make 'content' linear.

When we are reading, yes, we turn the pages, and the pages follow in an orderly fashion, but in our minds, we are moving around, and generally we don't finish a book in one sitting. This is a good thing – we are letting the text act on us more slowly. We are absorbing it. Then it is part of our private library.

The reason fiction is so good at moving around in time – compressing or expanding normal, linear time – is that our creative minds are not linear. We are always simultaneously journeying between past and future. The present is often provisional – we don't understand it till it's over.

Fiction works with this truth about our non-linear minds. So does poetry, that might take a single memory or insight and hold it for us so that it seems to stretch across far more time than the space it occupies.

Memory is not just 'what has happened' in the strict and factual sense. Two people in the same place at the same time will remember differently, not because we are unreliable narrators at a crime scene, but because what is significant means something different to us all.

A memory is not an artifact in a glass case at a museum. What is important about the memory changes as we do – a memory might fade, strengthen, suddenly return. It's a dynamic process.

Our own memories are not orderly. They/we are not alphabetical.

Memories don't sit chronologically like a diary entry. Memories sit side by side according to *emotional* resonance.

This is why something that happened yesterday will trigger something that happened five – or fifty – years ago.

Here's a piece I love. It's from a poem by the Irish poet W. B. Yeats. It's called 'The Municipal Gallery Revisited' (1937).

The poet is walking around an art gallery looking at the usual oil paintings of important, now mostly forgotten, figures.

Then . . .

> *Before a woman's portrait suddenly I stand;*
> *Beautiful and gentle in her Venetian way.*
> *I met her all but fifty years ago*
> *For twenty minutes in some studio.*
>
> *III*
> *Heart smitten with emotion I sink down,*
> *My heart recovering with covered eyes;*

Many of us have had the physical, literal experience, described by Paul Simon – *I met my old lover on the street last night.*

In the Yeats poem, we are upheld in the overwhelming power of this memory – a recall that for a time obliterates the present. The mind does more than witness reality; the mind is its own reality – and that reality is not an illusion.

Remember the end of David Nicholls' *One Day*. Dexter takes his daughter to Arthur's Seat in Edinburgh, Scotland, to recall the twenty years ago that he met Emma. Emma is dead. I don't think humans can, or should, only live in the present, even though the present is all we have. There's a psychological balance between the sane mantra of Buddhism – Be Here

Now – and the power of memory to reconnect us to the entirety of our lives.

Living in the past is not a recipe for mental health. But neither is the false forgetting of what is too painful to remember.

Fiction and poetry, music and theatre, offer safe and protected spaces where we can find our own memories – our own pasts – not in a documentary style way – *this is what happened to me* – but using the past in an allusive or symbolic way. That's what I did in *Oranges Are Not the Only Fruit*. It's not me but it is an avatar of me.

For women, fiction written by men is not always a safe place. Women characters in fiction written by men do seem to die more often than is statistically likely – something I noticed as a teenager, reading in secret, and wondering why this might be. I hadn't come across opera then . . . the stage is littered with dead females.

For so long, men wrote nearly all of what we read, see, or hear, and habits die hard. It's easier to kill the female than to break the habit of many lifetimes. That would mean giving women autonomy and equality. It would mean allowing women a soul not in service to the Hero journey.

When the Hero dies, it is often as a sacrifice for the good of all – his death is part of his heroism. He is remembered as much more than a love interest.

Women? RIP.

In the *Nights*, Shahrazad knows well that women are powerless in society and that their soon-to-be-forgotten deaths will likely be at the hands of some angry male who doesn't appreciate their behaviour.

As Shahrazad's stories progress, she relies on our memory of what we have heard previously so that she can build an invisible world that is complex and questioning. She never preaches or moralises; she doesn't judge, although her characters do, and we do. She lays out her carpet of stories, piece by piece, and we, the listener, the reader, will come to see something greater than the outcome of each story as it stands alone. She is making patterns.

Patterns are not the same as rules. Patterns are not statistics either. The Arab world loves patterns – look at their rugs and their architecture – but these patterns are often abstract – deliberately avoiding representation – especially representation of what is considered to be in the realm of the divine.

Both Islam and Judaism have a prohibition against idols, or graven images, the making of a totem to represent what cannot be represented. Representation is too obvious, too basic, too literal.

There is a historical sense here – if you are trying to distinguish your new religion/deity from all the other versions, it's a bold move to declare that yours cannot be known via any human-made depiction.

This Otherness roared back into Christianity during the Reformation. All that Catholic paraphernalia – the statues, the shrines, the relics, the icons, the amulets, the vestments, the altar furniture, the paintings, even the stained glass windows, had to go. The ultimate clearance is a Puritan wearing black and white, sitting in a bare New England chapel, with the sun shining through an open window.

Of course, refusing the paraphernalia around worship, because it's a distraction, soon morphs into a hatred of material excess of any kind.

Every so often, and usually through religion or art – think Quaker, Shaker, clean spare Modernism and Minimalism – humans just have to get rid of representing themselves – their inner selves – via stuff.

I won't call it a fashion. It's much more than a fashion. Humans keep trying to get closer to an essence – whether it's the essence of God, in whose image we are said to be made, or the essence of us. The shakeouts are always a repudiation of excess. This can be a sham, of course, as the ultra-wealthy can seem to live simply, though they do not. The toil of others is what their simple life depends upon.

Nevertheless, whether it's the princely Siddhartha Gautama, who walked out of his palaces to found Buddhism, or Saint Francis of Assisi, who gave away his wealth to be closer to God, or Moses, raised as a prince in Egypt, turning his back on safety and riches, material excess is equated with a lack of imagination.

Think of it as a Mar-a-Lago of the Mind.

Shahrazad's tales, stuffed with detail, unravelling, tumbling over each other, growing taller in the telling like the jinn who so often appear, are not minimalist. What's not in these stories? Stories piled on stories. A bazaar of excess. Wealth beyond the reach of avarice. Palaces that can't be counted. More diamonds than stars. It's an inventory of bling.

Or . . .

Look closer.

The message of the *Nights*, regardless of what story we

are reading, is the sovereignty of imagination. The people who come off badly in the *Nights* are those, rich or poor, clever or not, who can't see past their own representation of reality. They will always be poor, no matter how rich they are, because their heads are tuned to one TV channel.

Fortune or misfortune in the *Nights* happens to us all. Grifters or grafters. Callous or kind. Self-aware or self-involved. Good luck and bad luck. That's the baseline. Now what?

The *Nights* is counselling us not to get lost in the literal.

Those palaces, that wealth, the dancing girls, the camels, the chests of gold, look again and it's all vanished. In the *Nights*, treasure vanishes as often as it materialises. Look again, and there it is – piled high, ten times as much. Fabulous in the true meaning of the word; that is, it has no basis in reality.

It's what we read in the story Plato tells, in the *Republic* (*c.*380 BCE), of the captives in the cave who imagine that the shadows they see, cast by firelight, are the real and true world. Their heads facing only one way, their bodies shackled, they depend on their 'reality' to be 'real'.

But it is not.

Shakespeare is saying much the same thing through Prospero in *The Tempest* (1610).

> *Our revels now are ended. These our actors,*
> *As I foretold you, were all spirits, and*
> *Are melted into air, into thin air;*
> *And, like the baseless fabric of this vision,*
> *The cloud-capp'd towers, the gorgeous palaces,*

The solemn temples, the great globe itself,
Yea, all which it inherit, shall dissolve,
And, like this insubstantial pageant faded,
Leave not a rack behind. We are such stuff
As dreams are made on; and our little life
Is rounded with a sleep.

What we think is real isn't reality.

The invisible, unfettered, unbounded, non-material life of the imagination, and what it invents, *that* is the basis of reality. Not 'stuff'. Shakespeare and Shahrazad agree with Plato on this.

Shahrazad's insight into what is real and what is not, allows her to see past the daily death-cult of the Sultan. That's all he has – day in day out, another beheading. In Shahrazad's mind, his is the illusion. Hers will become the reality.

What is real?

What is an illusion?

Story by story, Shahrazad asks that question. Rather, she asks us to answer that question, and it's not easy. The patterns she weaves from her multi-threaded mind allow the reader to make patterns of their own. This is more than the content of each story. What is it about? That's too threadbare. What is it not about? That's a better question.

The experience of reading the *Nights*, its refusal to be compressed or explained, its bursting out at the seams, its lack of timidity, its deceptive simplicity, its beautiful complexity, is a primer for everything else of worth that we will read as life passes. Our reading builds our private library, and the connections, the patterns, are like tree roots spreading unseen, underground.

Yes, here are the trees, separate, seemingly unrelated, yet underneath is a vast rootal network.

The more you read the more connected your network. Not the superficial connections of the social network, rather the particular and personal connections you have made that form a vast raft beneath you.

In your mind you can cross-reference. In your mind you can see the pattern clearly. How something from Shakespeare fits with a story by A. M. Homes or George Saunders. Or a song by Joni Mitchell, or a painting where a line from a poem joins it to some place deep in you. This pattern you are making is unique. It is riches. It is yours. Here are palaces and jewels and jinn in jars. And they don't vanish at daybreak.

What do you remember? What is it that is invisible to others but vivid to you? Your private acres where you walk undisturbed by the buyers and sellers of the day? The portal back through time.

Fiction is odd because it deals in the invented memories of invented lives, yet its artifice brings us more vividly to an understanding – perhaps a reconciliation, sometimes a renunciation – of memories of our own. We believe our lives actually happened. Perhaps they did. What we have read did not happen – at least not in the same way – and yet each becomes a commentary on the other. My life on what I have read. What I have read on my life.

Shahrazad is correct. It becomes more difficult, or less important, to untangle these threads that bind together what we read and what we did. Or between one kind of fiction (our reality) and the fiction that explores such realities.

There's a novel I love by the British writer Vita Sackville-West, one-time lover of Virginia Woolf and the model for Woolf's time-travelling trans novel, *Orlando* (1928).

All Passion Spent (1931) follows the final years of Lady Slane, after the death of her husband, and the various attempts by her odious and inadequate children to try to force her out of the independence she finally wants for herself.

Lady Slane meets the art collector Mr FitzGeorge, who starts coming round for tea, and one day reminds Lady Slane that they have met before – in India, when he was a young man on his travels, and she was the wife of the Viceroy.

All of this had been forgotten by Lady Slane. She must retrace her steps back through time, to a young woman with a new baby in the troubling splendour of the Raj. Her every wish was at her command. Yet, the memory is not agreeable at first, as her past returns, no longer in clichés, or official accounts, or formal photographs, or the sanctified memories of others.

Now, while she sits staring at the strange old man arrived like a figure of Destiny, she feels keenly what she lost, what she sacrificed, to live that polished perfect life, her husband's life, and his life only.

FitzGeorge has been in love with Lady Slane for more than fifty years. He never married. Suddenly he says to her:

Face it, Lady Slane. Your children. Your husband, your splendour, were nothing but obstacles that kept you from yourself... You were too young, I suppose, to know any better, but when you chose that life, you sinned against the light.

It is a powerful denouncement but a welcome one.

The clock above the mantlepiece ticks. Time need not have the final word.

Now, the conversation can change – because the people holding the conversation can acknowledge what was buried/lost/distorted when so confidently narrated as a story where they were characters, and not authors.

It's a conversation that began fifty years ago.

Sometimes, if we are lucky, we will resume a vital conversation before it is too late. It doesn't matter that it is too late to change the circumstances of the past, or to change our choices – that's the mundane plane, the land of the everyday, and on the mundane plane, yes, we run out of time.

It's too late can be a tragedy, or it can be a matter-of-fact statement.

Spiritually we don't run out of time. Truth matters, and it matters that what is important has been understood – by oneself, certainly, and perhaps by others.

The illusion is done. Reality begins.

Shaken though she was, Lady Slane laughed frankly. She felt immensely grateful to the outrageous old man.
    He says:
    Now we can be friends.

Shahrazad notices that morning is coming. Her story begins to end so that it can begin again.

*

Out in the desert, the Ifrit is satisfied. An excellent story. A proper exchange for one third of the merchant's blood.

The Ifrit gets up and picks up his sword to behead the trembling merchant.

By now though, there is a second man at the scene. He saunters into the shady grove, walking two Salukis on gold braided leads.

'Ifrit!' he says. 'That is one story, I have another. If it is more marvellous yet, will I take a second share in the blood of this man?'

The Ifrit orders the merchant to kneel in preparation for death.

The dogs cower.

'Well?' says the man. 'Do you want to hear this story or not?'

Saluki x 2. Golden collars. Sight hounds. Fast runners. Hard to train.

These dogs are hunters, and they hunt what their eyes can see. They were bred and prized in what Europeans used to call the Fertile Crescent of the Middle East. In between the rivers Tigris and Euphrates. Along the banks of the River Jordan. Where life and learning came to be before it came to be anywhere else. Settled farming. The first library in the world. Not parchment. Not scrolls. Not bound pages. Clay tablets. The same method that Yahweh used when He wrote out the Ten Commandments for Moses. This library was built in the great city of Nineveh. You remember Nineveh – where Jonah was swallowed by the Whale.

But this isn't a story about whales. (Yet.)
It's a story about dogs.
These two dogs?
Yes.
What are they doing here?
I'm about to tell you.
They just look like dogs to me.
What we can see is never the whole story.
What are you talking about?
Sit under the trees and listen.

Once upon a time, these two dogs were the human brothers of the man who now leads them. Their father died and divided his living between all three. Only one of the brothers worked hard.

The other two spent what they had. Nowhere to be seen as their brother did his best and built a business.

And then they returned.

More than once.

More than once this good man shares what he has with them. They bow, they thank him, they go their separate ways.

Again, they return as beggars.

This time, he travels with them and equips a ship. Goods bought and sold. Everyone likes this man because he is honest. People trust him.

The dart-eyed brothers watch how it's done. They try to copy him. Everyone knows they are frauds.

Never mind. What does it matter? It's been a spectacular trip. Ship laden with treasure. More booty than anyone needs. Lifetimes of ease floating over the waves to go home.

No one needs anything any more. They are all rich men.

But the brothers in human form sit up in the ship night after night, talking and drinking. They are envious. They want everything for themselves. As long as their brother is alive, what is the truth? The truth is that they are a pair of losers. Once he is gone, they can claim all the success, all the prestige. It's never about money. Not by now.

They drink some more and gaze at the black sea. They plot to throw him overboard while he sleeps. Him and his wife who loves him. Yes, on their travels, he met a woman and fell in love. It's revolting.

Why should he have it all? Money and love.

They are jealous of love, only able to buy its counterfeit from the girls with kohl round their eyes. Love like that comes expensive. They don't understand that what is freely given cannot be bought.

They have already slipped a sleeping draught into the wine they all shared at dinner.

Hold the lantern. Creep down into the bowels of the boat. Pick them up, one each, how light they are. Perhaps because they carry no guilt.

Ready?

SLOSH!

SLOSH!

Down into the Deep goes their good and kind brother and his loving wife. He wakes, breathing salt water, fighting for his life, his body is marshalled by fishes. The ship must be sinking, he thinks. Is this how it ends?

It's not ended yet.

He feels two strong arms wrapped around him, and

suddenly he's in the air, water drops flying off him like sparks as he is carried to an island where he will be safe.

He lands so gently, the way you settle a child, and his wet feet are covered in sand.

There's his wife, but she is and isn't his wife. She looks like his wife, but she is huge, and her body is glowing.

Oh... OK...

He realises that his wife is no mortal woman. She is an Ifrita. She has saved them both. But now, she wants her revenge.

Already, he is pleading for them, already, he begs her to change her mind. Don't kill them!

She passes her hand over his eyes and he falls asleep. She covers him with her cloak.

She knows what to do.

Since these brothers in human form are greedy for what they can see, let them become sighthounds. Let them see what will never be theirs again – a strong upright body. Let them learn what it is to be loyal.

Meanwhile, the brothers in human form have sailed home. As they hurry down the gangplank laden with treasure, each feels his arms lengthening, his spine shortening, his legs contracting. Skin grows hair, tongue is long and pinky brown. Each turns to speak and there is only a whine and a bark.

The men unloading the ship run away in terror, and soon it is decreed that all the goods brought home in triumph must be stored away, and only enough spent to feed the brothers, now in dog-form, one meal of meat every day.

Clean water and straw are arranged in a small lean-to against their brother's shop. Surely, he will come home and all will be understood?

A woman combs their fur once a week.

By a series of adventures and devices, the good man does make his way home, and when he arrives in Baghdad, there, outside his shuttered shop, are two Saluki hounds in fancy collars.

He recognises them at once. He knows what is real and what is its counterfeit.

He changes their water. They trot beside him to the butcher. This, then, is life.

Time passes. It always does. Nothing changes. Why would it?

The hounds seem content to be with him. Yet, this good man remains troubled in spirit.

He never wanted adventure. Had no wish to make difficult decisions. All he wanted was to make a life. He's read about heroes and he isn't one of those. He wonders how he ever came to marry an Ifrita? Why would a being like her want an ordinary man like him?

And where is she? He misses her.

After a year and a day, he decides to travel again to seek out his wife.

Not trusting the ocean, he journeys by foot, his brothers in animal-form by his side.

And here he is.

Listening to this story, in the desert, the merchant who will soon die nods his head. He understands. The old man understands too.

But the bloodthirsty Ifrit waves his scimitar and asks the traveller, 'Why would you aid such worthless creatures?'

The good man bows his head. There is no answer but one.

'Love. The most potent shape-shifter in the world. Love that changes you. Love that changes me. Love that finds forgiveness where there is none.'

The Ifrit lowers his sword.

The *Nights* is as bleak a beginning as a mind can invent. A woman is filibustering for her life, preventing the final decision that will bring about her death, and only her wits can save her.

This is not a love story.

Or is it?

The shape-shifting stories we encounter at the start of the *Nights* revolve around love's failures.

Love fails in myriad ways. Humans cheat, lie, betray, disappoint, wound, exploit, flee, refuse the responsibilities that walk alongside love. And yet, in every culture, across time, love is offered as the highest value. I don't mean love as romantic love only. I mean the love of a mother for her children. Of a patriot for their country. Of a campaigner for a cause – even if the outcome is imprisonment or death.

All religions call themselves religions of love – though they have a history, and a perpetual present tense, of persecuting anyone who disagrees with them.

That's a strange kind of love.

Shahryar is a man stinging from love's smarts. Did he love his unfaithful wife? Who knows? What we do know is that his self-love is unopposed. The prime problem with power is that it lives in a palace where there are no mirrors. Self-reflection is the first casualty of omnipotence. Love is next.

The Sultan is as far away from love as any man can be when the *Nights* opens. His bloodthirsty battle is against love itself. Having been betrayed he must dig a moat of blood around his heart. His nightly sex-acts with a trembling teenager are not the actions of a man who wants any woman to fall in love with him. Why should a woman, any woman, bother to save such a man? Save him from himself? He doesn't deserve it.

Yet, as Shahrazad's endeavour unfolds, she will save Shahryar, as well as the women and girls whose lives depend on her success.

Saving Shahryar from his own empty heart is not Shahrazad's intention, at least at the start.

But that is the way with stories. They know more than we do. They do more than we know.

WHAT YOU RISK REVEALS WHAT YOU VALUE

A Fisherman went down to the shore. He had a routine. He was a methodical man.

He cast his net four times a day and was satisfied with whatever he caught. He needed to feed his family and turn a little cash.

That morning the sky was dark. The sea was choppy. He had to hurry. He knew the sea as well as he knew his own family. Its moods, discontents, the easy days when the fish jumped into the net. Today, the waves were quick and spiteful, slapping at his bare legs. He waded in, and threw from the shoulder, watching the much-mended net sink, until he could tug it a little.

What's this?

His net had caught something heavy. He hauled and struggled and finally landed the catch.

Damn! Dead donkey.

Go again.

Another long line with a flick of the wrist this time. The net went further.

Now what?

The net is straining. Something is in there. He turns away dragging the net from behind. In the shallows he examines the catch.

What is the point of life? There's nothing here but dirty sacks bulging with wet sand.

Third time lucky.

This time he wades deeper. The shallow waters are too murky. But out there – yes, he can see a glint. It's a shoal of fish. It's a hit!

He loves the shining water and the size of the world.

He pulls and tugs and tugs and pulls and feels his shoulders heating up. His feet are deep-sunk in the moving sand.

He drags the net back to the shore as best he can, seeing that it's torn in places, though not by the weight of the shoal. This treasure of his is nothing more than rusty tin and ships' waste tangled in the weave.

This is the story of his life. A lot of work for next to nothing.

He's going home.

As he bundles the sullen net, he remembers he's thrown three times, and so, he must throw once more. That's the deal. He made this deal with himself, and he honours it, because if you can't keep a promise to yourself, what promises can you keep?

Right, he says, I will go home with nothing, and the children will be hungry tonight, but I will go home with my self-respect.

His net is so torn that he doesn't cast it. Instead, he takes off his clothes and swims into the sand-swelled water. He can't see an inch beneath the troubled surface and it's starting to thunder on the horizon.

He lets the net sink. All he needs is a turtle coming in for shelter.

At once his net catches on a weight. Not too heavy. Not

too light. He slips and swallows salt water. He returns to the shore, dragging the heavy thing behind him.

Turtle, for sure, he says. We can eat it. Turtle blood is sweet. Turtle soup is good.

Naked, on shore, his fingers numb with salt and cuts, he gets a knife from his clothes and cuts the net even more to retrieve the object. The net will have to be remade for tomorrow anyway, but his son can do that.

The object is interesting – it is encrusted with barnacles and sea-growth, but he can see it's not a turtle. He can see that it's a jar. A bit of scraping with the knife, and he scratches through barnacles to brass.

Brass!

Glory Be! This will sell in the metals market and give him enough money for a week. He thanks Allah for reminding him not to give up.

Out of defeat comes victory, he says, adding every other platitude he has ever heard . . . Dark night new dawn . . . sorrow before joy . . . loss is the beginning of love . . . failure today victory tomorrow . . .

And all the while he is scraping away with his little knife, and there is a seal at the mouth of the jar, and as he polishes it clean with his tatty jacket, he sees the Seal of Solomon.

This is a prize.

Not noticing the sky is blacker. Not noticing the waves the height of houses. Not noticing his shivering body. He picks at the lid until he loosens it enough to pop the knife-blade underneath.

Here we go!

Jewels! Gold!

No . . . steam . . . what? Thick steam like the boiler that heats the water for the ritual baths. This steam is red and blue. It's thicker than steam. It's a vapour that's turning into a solid. It reaches the sky dense as a tornado, but he can't see so high, all he can see is a huge pair of bare feet. Calves like tree trunks. Thighs like hills.

He crouches, head down, trembling.

A hand reaches down and scoops him up. He's held like a sparrow under the red eyes of an Ifrit.

'Slave!' shouts the Ifrit. 'I am going to kill you. Choose how you want to die!'

The Fisherman is trembling so much he can barely speak.

Nevertheless, indignation overcomes terror.

He says: 'Ifrit! I have set you free! Why would you return harm for kindness?'

The Ifrit replies: 'Slave! I have lived in that disgusting jar for eighteen hundred years. When King Solomon himself imprisoned me there, I vowed to serve faithfully the first person who set me free.

'After five hundred years, I vowed to heap riches on whoever set me free.

'After another five hundred years, I promised three wishes to whoever would set me free.

'Now, too much time has passed, and I have vowed to kill whoever sets me free – as my revenge on my punishment.'

'I did not punish you!' cried the Fisherman.

'I don't care!' said the Ifrit. 'Prepare to die.'

The Fisherman found his mind was suddenly as still and clear as the sea below him was frothy and troubled. He had one chance. His wits.

He said, 'Ifrit! I accept my fate. Put me down and lie on the sand with the jar between us.'

The earth shook as the Ifrit lay down, his legs and torso stretching to the next village. His great arms were at right angles to his huge head. His eyes gleamed.

The Fisherman picked up the jar and examined it.

'Ifrit! You claim you were imprisoned in this jar, and yet, not even your hands clasped together in prayer would fit inside. By the Prophet, you are lying to me! You have appeared out of nowhere to lie to me.'

The Ifrit roared with rage. 'How dare you accuse me of lying?'

'Well, then,' said the Fisherman, 'kill me however you like, but first, on this Seal of Solomon, grant my dying wish, and prove to me that you came out of this jar!'

The Ifrit was frightened by the mention of the Seal of Solomon, and besides, he was vain, also he had not spoken to anyone for eighteen hundred years, and so he had forgotten how it's done. It didn't occur to him that this might be the cunning voice of a double-tongue.

Avoiding discussion, he stood up and stamped his foot.

'Slave! Prepare to die . . . but first . . .'

The Ifrit began to spin like a whirlwind, faster and faster, his rainbow colours blending to white, then the white of him shedding sparks, and as he blazed, he became less solid, more like a burning, transparent shimmering veil, and then the veil was sucked inside the jar so that only a bubbling popping froth remained on the top.

Fast as thought, the Fisherman grabbed the seal with Solomon's mark on it and shoved it into the neck of the jar. Then he sat on the jar praying to God to save him.

The Ifrit realised what had happened. The jar shook so hard with his wails that the Fisherman feared the worst. But the seal was magic and so the Ifrit could not escape.

'Ifrit! This is what you deserve for wishing to do harm to one who was innocent!'

Shahrazad breaks off her story. Morning is visible on the horizon.

A recurring theme of the *Nights* is harm done to those who are innocent. This is aimed, first of all, at the murderous Sultan Shahryar, busily blaming all women for the actions of his wife.

But everything the Sultan hears, we hear. What he must consider, we must consider.

Shahryar's war on women is still underway. The freedoms won by women, over the last 120 years or so, in the West, have ignited a blaze of rage among insecure men who can't accept that biology isn't destiny.

Physical, verbal, political and legal attacks on a woman's right to be herself, and to exercise agency in the world, are rising at a frightening rate.

Yet, when we read the rants of well-funded white males, like those behind the USA's Project 2025 (contraception is a 'snake strangling the American family', Kevin Roberts), or contemplate the millions of teenage boys who follow wealthy women-haters online, or listen to the whines of incels, and misnamed pro-lifers, and watch with horror at what is happening to women and girls in Afghanistan under the Taliban and women and girls in 'modern' Turkey, where domestic violence is running at 40 per cent of all women (source: *Human Rights Watch 2022*), what do we conclude?

Gender war is the oldest war in the world. And the most dangerous. More than half of the world is female. The only way to discriminate against a majority of that size is to use basic biology to justify baseless ideology. What follows is what we know – restrictions on behaviour, education and opportunity. Pseudo-scientific rationale for the bogus, second-class status of women, solemnly presented as only what nature intended. Accepting this nonsense makes it easy to cross the line from gender stereotypes into racial stereotypes.

Religion has form on supporting both sets of prejudice, plus an all too quick discrimination against anyone, male or female, who worships a different sky-god, or none.

Why are humans always looking for a fight?

In America, freedom of worship and religious tolerance was a cornerstone of independence – wanting such freedom of worship, and the life it would entail, was why the Puritan Fathers sailed across the ocean from England in 1630.

It's true that they didn't have tolerance for anything, or anyone who wasn't part of their cult, but by the time of the Declaration of Independence (1776), new-found Americans were optimistic of a broader, less hierarchical, more inclusive country. Not for indigenous people or people of colour or women – progress is slow – but theirs was a pioneering template for human choices – and we should recognise that, just as they tried to recognise the sovereignty of each individual. Here, at last, was a republic where anyone who worked hard and had their wits about them could rightfully expect to forge a decent life. A life not dependent on the lottery of birth. *No rich man in his castle no poor man at his gate.*

At the time this was not a fantasy.

Americans still believe that theirs is the land of opportunity, but the radical-Right, and conspicuously the religious Right, do not extend this offer to build your own life in your own way, to anyone outside of an increasingly narrow and intolerant view of race, gender and human nature.

A slogan caught my eye recently. Yes, evangelicals love a slogan – our house was wallpapered with them. You know the kind of thing: Seek The Lord. Watch and Pray. Think of God not the Dog (one of Mrs Winterson's). The slogan I saw said: *Tolerance is not a Commandment.*

I was taken aback by this permission to hate.

Tolerance. What does that mean?

Tolerance is the capacity to live and let live when it comes to opinions and behaviours we don't share. Accept difference. Look for what is good in the person you disagree with. Remember that you are not perfect, and that you and your beliefs are not the Gold Standard for others. We're not talking about bashing old ladies over the head, or abusing kids, or disrespecting communal public spaces, or breaking the law. We must all obey the law if we want to live in a safe and civil society. Tolerance is the grey area. It's where we exercise restraint. We're talking about everyday give and take, culturally, generationally, with regard to sexual orientation, and whether you have a faith, or none.

A little bit of Let It Be.

For Christians, tolerance is right there in the Second Commandment:

Isn't it?
Love Thy Neighbour As Thyself.

I agree. It's hard. It's the hardest challenge there is. In Islam, this is jihad. The struggle against the lower self. Trying to do good. Not harming others. Showing understanding instead of anger. Or, if anger is appropriate, looking for solutions, not just punishments.

In Islam, the greater jihad is always this wrestle with the self. The ultimate battle. Making it about sex, drugs and rock 'n' roll is too easy. Making it about the infidel is too easy. All religions love to hate the infidel – the one who isn't of the faith. While we are beating them up, we don't have to worry about ourselves. The reason God's kingdom is not on earth is all the fault of the 'others' – and when we've killed them, or locked them up, or deported them, or forced them to convert, all will be well.

Sound familiar?

Politics is just the same. The state of things is always someone else's fault.

Hitler called the Jews 'parasites', 'lice', 'vermin'. Vermin is a word Donald Trump has used too, when describing those he labels the 'radical left lunatics'. Or people with 'bad genes'.

In 1955, the East German Stasi, the secret police, worked undercover to remove activists away from the border with West Germany. They named their efforts Operation Vermin.

Mao Zedong called his political opponents 'poisonous weeds'.

Netanyahu insists that genocide in Gaza is in defence of Western civilisation against 'terrorists'.

Babies and children are not terrorists.

*

The enemy is not just/always/only on the outside. The enemy is within. What kind of a person are you? What do you value? What will you fight for? And who is in charge inside the 'you' so confidently targeting 'them' as the problem?

There are plenty of enemies on the outside – our neglectful/nasty parents maybe, our psycho boss, our controlling partner – these figures are horrible enough in the flesh, but their real power is when they live, uninvited and unwanted, rent-free, in our minds. It's when, and because, we internalise these baleful bullies that their power ruins the bright spirit that we are – or could be.

No matter what your campaign is out in the world, no matter how successful you are in life, there is a battle that someday comes back to its source.

The self.

My mother was an introverted and unhappy woman who couldn't look at her own life, in all its misery and loss. She preferred to look at everyone else's life. And blame them.

It was an ultra-religious evangelical home, and Mrs Winterson couldn't tolerate anyone. Especially not her neighbours.

There is a line in the book of Isaiah about God blotting them out – meaning our sins, so it's optimistic, in a way. For Mrs W, it wasn't about sins – it was about the people of the world. God would Blot Them Out.

She longed for the Second Coming – the Best Day Ever in the Barbie movie version of the evangelical church calendar. After that, every day would be exactly like every other day, and no one would be unhappy or die, or have flat feet, or a flat car battery, because all the enemies, all the 'others', would finally be wiped out.

By Mrs W's reckoning, the godless lived along our whole street, and some of them weren't married, and some had no jobs, and some had a record player with the Rolling Stones blasting too loud, reminding her she could get no satisfaction, and the one with the rosary hanging in the window was a Catholic, and some were childless cat ladies.

A trip down to the town meant a Dante-style journey through various circles of Hell (on Earth).

Past Woolworths. 'A Den of Vice'. Past Marks and Spencer. 'The Jews killed Christ.' Past the funeral parlour and the pie shop. 'They share an oven.' Past the biscuit stall and its moon-faced owners. 'Incest.' Past the pet parlour. 'Bestiality.' Past the bank. 'Usury.' Past the Citizen's Advice Bureau. 'Communists'. Past the Day Nursery. 'Unmarried mothers.' Past the hairdresser. 'Vanity.'

I don't think she had read Jean-Paul Sartre's play, *No Exit*, but she would agree with Sartre that Hell is Other People.

Didn't matter – the Incinerator of Judgement would be firing up anytime soon.

In the New Testament, a smart-ass lawyer asks Jesus what the Second Commandment means: Who is my neighbour? This person I should love? Not just love . . . but love the way I love myself?

Jesus tells the famous story of the Good Samaritan. A guy has been beaten and robbed. Everybody passing by does their best to do nothing – they complain about the violence these days, the way things are on the streets, no law and order, and they all walk by on the other side. Except the person from Samaria – a low-grade hole where nice folks don't live. This person aids the beaten-up guy and gets him to an inn where he can rest, and he pays for what is needed.

Jesus is saying that anyone who needs my help is my neighbour. It might be material help, it might be acceptance, it might be a handshake across the divide, it might be welcoming the unwelcome.

What the story shows us is that this isn't the usual response. It's easier to tut and headshake and do nothing. Or blame.

If you are thinking, somewhere: it's their own fault/what do they expect/dressed like that/kissing in public/abaya on abaya off/should speak English/should go home/this is a big city, wise up/I am in a hurry – then we reduce our common humanity to a checklist of who deserves our tolerance, our helping hand, and who doesn't. The Victorians did it handsomely with their Deserving and Undeserving Poor.

Shahrazad's *Nights* start with wrong done to those who don't deserve it. Jesus's story shows a material wrong done to someone who doesn't deserve it. Too often we justify ourselves when we actively wrong someone, or passively don't help someone. We do it by trying to prove to ourselves that, well, maybe they did deserve what happened.

We see this all the time when it comes to violence against women. Did she provoke? What was she wearing? Is she seeing someone else?

Is she pretty? Is she ugly? Did she ignore you? She's a dyke. She only got hired because she's a woman.

Or, we could take the extreme view of Shahryar, that all women 'deserve' to be punished, because all women are like this.

*

Mozart's opera: *Cosi Fan Tutte* (1790). That's what it means. They're all the same.

Mozart was not a radical, and certainly not a radical feminist, and neither was his librettist Da Ponte. They were men of their time. Yet, what was written as a comic opera – where it's proved beyond doubt that women cannot be trusted – has survived the centuries to reveal a different view of women (and men) that really is radical.

Women are not wagers at the gaming table. Love is not a bet between bros. Faithfulness is a contract – that is, there is more than one party to the agreement. Cynical old men are not to be trusted with what they envy (romance and youth).

If you don't know the story – here it is:

Ferrando and Guglielmo love Dorabella and Fiordiligi. Old louche, Don Alfonso, prevails on the young men to pretend to go to war, then to return secretly and in disguise, as a pair of strangers, to see if they can woo each other's girlfriends. Women are the same the world over, declares Don Alfonso, a faithful one is as rare as the mythical phoenix.

The foolish young men agree to the wager. What happens when they return in disguise is funny, but upsetting, as each of the women, for different reasons and in different ways, gradually falls for her new suitor.

There's nothing in the story, or the wager, about the reality of soldiering life. The women know there are sex workers in every garrison town. Everyone knows that these heart-on-sleeve men would not be faithful to their faraway fiancées for five minutes. But the men would think nothing of it, and expect these soon-to-be wives to think nothing of it either.

Now, for us, as moderns, watching this opera, it seems far sadder than it would have done when gendered behaviour was just a fact of life – *what is* – or God-given, whatever god you choose.

Now, what do we see? We see men putting women to the test, while submitting to no such test themselves. We see the women flattered to be given real attention for once. To be wooed in their own right, not as suitable wives or trophies, but as human beings with complex feelings. And when – sort of – things come together at the end, and everyone is supposed to accept the bitter outcome of the game, we don't laugh. How can we? All four young people have been broken.

The strangest thing of all, at least to me, is that when the opera opens, it is the women who are pretending – going through all the motions, trotting out all the lines, painting their nails, sighing, checking for a message, and looking forward to being tradwives. The boys are just, well, being boys. Men have characters. Women have clichés.

But later, as the story unfolds, when it is the boys who are playing a part in disguise, the two young women are able to become themselves. Who they really are and not the same as each other at all – in fact, they don't have much in common. The clichés stop. They speak from their hearts – not from what they ought to say. This is the real unmasking.

It's an absolute reversal and it's shocking.

Do I think Mozart/Da Ponte meant this?

Absolutely not! They were having fun and making music. *Cosi* is not written as Woke. I am not injecting it with Woke.

But what we discover so often with art, any art, any art form, is that as it lives on, surviving the tests of time, subsequent audiences see and hear and understand things differently, because society has altered. The work is the same. It's us who have changed. What I am suggesting isn't to force a view, or to read what isn't there – we are discovering richness that is in there from the start, because the art is always bigger than the artist. Always bigger than its moment in time.

This is a strange truth.

It's why it's pointless to cancel writers/artists whose personal views, in their own time, are troubling to us now. We're not marrying them. We aren't hoping to make a new best friend. We're not swiping left or right. The work itself is not confined to the mind, or the morals, of the person who made it.

Sometimes, in a stage show, a director might bring out something that hasn't been seen in earlier productions. It can be gratuitous – and I hate that – it's just attention-seeking, and usually an easy way out. It's a failure to read deep enough to find what is likely there in abundance anyway.

When the newness we see is found from within, and we recognise it, that's unsettling. Especially if we think we know the piece so well.

Do we?

I love new work. It's oxygen. But it's equally important to experience life outside of what is contemporary, beyond whatever is new on the stands, and certainly beyond the news itself, because when we go back in time, through literature, or via any art, we are granted the power of double vision.

Simultaneously, we see that the past isn't the present, dressed up as costume drama, the past is *different*. The past is emphatically not now. That's my disappointment with so much 'content' costume drama on TV. It's not the past at all. Therefore, it takes us exactly nowhere but here.

The double vision advantage is this: while we do see the difference of the past – that it *really* isn't the present – we also see how hard it is for humans to let go of ideology masquerading as some sort of natural law. When the status quo changes, it doesn't happen out of nowhere; it takes work – huge work – whether it's civil rights, votes for women, trade unions, education for workers. This is more than costume drama. This is not a timeline of the forces of history – this is humans forcing history. It's crucial to know it, because in the here and now, we are not alone, isolated and bobbing about on the sea of time. We are connected to what has gone before. We are made by what has gone before. Who. What. Why. Where. When.

And all the changes that happen start to happen when a group of people open their minds to a different reality. *What if?*

Art opens our imagination. Being able to imagine what it is like to be someone else – including someone we would never want to know in real life – brings awareness of what is beyond our experience. There isn't time to experience very much in this life – and much of what we do experience just gets lost. Or, as the poet T. S. Eliot puts it: 'We had the experience but missed the meaning.'

Could be the poster for social media . . .

Art is there to focus our attention.

When I read, I get out of my current situation and inside a very different situation. It doesn't matter whether I identify or recoil. Whether I agree or I don't.

*

Reading the *Nights* is often bewildering. On the top line, the easy level, like humming the tune, are the stories you can read to your kids as well as tell around the campfire. When someone asks for a story, you know a few stories to tell.

But going below the surface, into the deep water that is the substance of these tales, is to meet the same kinds of dilemmas faced in our world, the same judgements, whether reckless or just. The balance between punishment and mercy.

Punishment, we all understand. Little kids do, when they hear the witch has been shoved in the oven, or the ogre's head has been chopped off. We cheer, and we like it.

Mercy, which follows from compassion, which follows from a deeper insight into human nature, is something we have to learn to understand. I think humans have an instinct to forgive; whether we do, whether we *should*, is an ethical issue. And it's complicated

What is forgiveness? Who deserves it? The religions of the world tell us that no one really deserves it, in the strict sense, yet God offers it and teaches it.

One of the most beautiful passages in the New Testament is the story of the Woman taken in Adultery. The Pharisees want to stone her – that's the penalty. Not for the man, of course, just the woman. Jesus answers their bloodlust with this. 'Let him who is without sin cast the first stone.'

The Taliban enjoys stoning women – but before we conclude that their version of Islam is disgusting, and Christian countries are wonderful, ask yourself about slut-shaming online, revenge porn, deepfakes, about the number of women killed by their ex-partners for finding another man, the violence against women that is really only now being seen for what it is: Terrorism.

Nathaniel Hawthorne wrote a book about this subject, set in Puritan New England. *The Scarlet Letter* (1850). Hester Prynne must wear her adulterous A around her neck forever. She is spurned by her community, even though it's the Pastor who was her lover. A story that is still current, still real. Taylor Swift put the line in her song 'Love Story'. *You were Romeo. I was a scarlet letter.*

With or without God, questions of forgiveness, mercy, compassion – these are lifetimes of questions.

Those closest to us often hurt us the most – or we hurt them – perhaps in thoughtless, self-entitled ways, perhaps deliberately, and for gain.

We meet such scenarios often, as the *Nights* builds, not because this is a textbook in why you should never trust the people closest to you, but to demonstrate that everyone, everywhere, is likely to be disappointed, let down, betrayed, or worse, by those we should be able to trust. Shahrazad is saying to Shahryar: 'It's not just you. You may be World King, but Cosi Fan Tutti (no feminine plural please, just the plural will do fine). Everyone is like this.'

When I was a young person, learning to navigate my world, I knew I could not trust the people closest to me – my mother and father.

My father was a good man but weak, and he was no match for my complicated, emotionally damaged mother.

I was a match for her, and that was the problem. I could never shut up and take it, whether 'it' was a beating (spare the rod and spoil the child), a piece of gnomic advice (never let a boy touch you down there), knees being a woman's zone of temptation, if I was following Mrs W's coordinates right. Then there were her bizarre rules around clothing (corduroy for boys, Crimplene for girls). Crimplene, bulked polyester fibre, was part of the craze for synthetic materials that started after the Second World War, along with acrylic, polyester, spandex, Terylene.

Mrs W loved a synthetic – quick drying and no ironing – and so all our bedclothes were nylon. Nylon is a 1930s product that caught on during the Second World War as a substitute for silk. Particularly for women's stockings. Mrs W thought nylon was glamorous because of the name. New York and London = Nylon. It's a fake etymology, but it convinced budget housewives seeking film star allure.

Nobody knew about microplastic pollution back then. Synthetics were the materials of the future.

The thing about the future is that so long as humans are part of it, the same old issues are always there – whether we are wearing animal skins or spandex. Crimplene or leather.

Doesn't matter whether you are Shahryar or Mrs Winterson. You or me. Then or now.

Who can I trust? Who loves me? Am I safe? These questions are so basic. When the answers are negative, tell me, how do you make a life?

I am not a suspicious type, but I was an anxious, frightened child who didn't know, couldn't know, that home should be a place of safety.

What I did discover, as I read books, was exactly what Shahrazad is trying to teach Shahryar: that cruel disappointment is universal, but it is not the only story.

*

When you are a child, you learn about love from your family. Where that fails, love will have to be relearned later. The alternative is tyranny. Tyranny over others, so that they bend to your will. And perhaps what is worse, tyranny over your own loving self, always trying to be heard and healed, a self that must be banished – banished for fear of more hurt. A tyrant is someone who is absolute and unrestrained.

In love, we are never absolute, because we must consider others.

In love, we are always restrained, because we will put others first.

In 1992, I wrote a novel called *Written on the Body*. Its opening line is: Why is the measure of love loss?

For me, love could only involve catastrophic loss. First, of my birth mother, who was doing her best, at not yet seventeen, and tried to throw me clear of the wreckage. On the adoption form she says, 'better for Janet to have a mother and a father.'

Single parents were seen as loose women. Children of single mothers were stigmatised. I have written that in the past tense, but if the retro-right-wingers in the USA and Europe gain more power, that's where we will be again. No abortions, restricted contraception, and stigma, not support, for single parents. By that, we mean women. Men are allowed to abandon their children. Mothers are the parent who is expected to stay.

My birth mother was pregnant with me before the Pill was available to unmarried women. You could say, and I do, that it's great that I am here. You could also say, and I do, that the situation my mother found herself in, at sixteen years old, wasn't the best thing for her.

She had to give me away, but when I met her, and I was

fifty by then, she told me she had thought of me all those years and always spent my birthday by herself. She had two other children who knew nothing of me.

I missed that mother of mine. The voice of her in the womb. The gait of her. When we met, we walked identically. How is that possible? The six weeks I had being breastfed by her were noted on my adoption form. 'Now on bottle.' I missed her smell. Her breathing. Her rough softness. Her physical size. Small and compact, like me.

The missingness of the missing. I didn't know what it was I was feeling, only that I felt it. Those feelings were not recognised, let alone understood, and so, I learned to hide feelings I couldn't manage, and that no one else wanted to know about.

It's what we do to survive.

Later, I learned to hide my excitement over the vast world opened up to me by reading. I learned to hide my emotional and sexual feelings for girls. I grew up thinking that life was a game of concealment.

In Britain in the 1960s, as in Europe, as in America, concealment of some kind was essential for many, especially women (hide your ambition, your discontent with life), especially gay people (hide your desire). Immigrants couldn't conceal themselves, so their only choice was assimilation or confrontation.

Not much of a choice.

Yet, change was coming. Pop culture, music culture, youth culture, the arts. Social democracy after the war, in much of Europe and in the USA, was pointing away from class hierarchies. Feminism began its work of dismantling the manmade hierarchies of gender. The Civil Rights movement, in the USA, forced white people to look squarely at their own prejudices. Old ways of thinking didn't fit the times any more.

I benefitted from that liberalisation. From free education, from opportunities for women, from money for the arts as part of national pride – what we all deserved, and not as luxury items for the rich.

Without those huge social changes happening around me, I couldn't have gone to study at the University of Oxford or made a life as a writer. I know my opportunities came from the political work of others, work that built an infrastructure for those who had always been left out: working people, people of colour, women of all colours, even posh women who had money and family but no independence.

Getting on in life is never just about talent and hard work.

I look back now, and wonder why nobody told me, when I opened my first bank account in 1979, that women in the UK had only been able to do that – without a male guarantor – for four years. I should have known that, aged nineteen.

My parents never had a bank account or a credit card. My dad was paid in cash. Maybe that's why I didn't know.

But then, nobody told me that the Oxford intake of females when I went up to study, stood at 30 per cent. At that time, only 14 per cent of young people, male or female, went to any university – the majority not from state schools. I had done well. Nobody told me that either.

But then, nobody told me you could buy fuel on a motorway – this was only my second trip on one – so I carried petrol in cans in the back of my van, so I could pull over and top up live, on the hard shoulder, with the engine running. Couldn't turn it off because the alternator was dodgy, and it might not start again.

Self-belief can get you a long way. I could tell the story of my life as one of the Seven Basic Plots. Rags to Riches. Poor Kid Makes Good.

All down to the individual! Society is free and fair!

Most people, certainly most women, have not made their living writing their own books in their own way, and are still doing so forty years after they began. So, I know that's an exception to the rule – and the Fairy Tale Right loves the exception to the rule.

But there's more to it than being an exception. Yes, I worked hard (Industry and Prudence Conquer) and I am bright, but outside of the me-ness of me, there was something else going on. Something much bigger than me. A road had opened up for my kind – working-class people, working-class women – a road as fabulous as anything Dorothy skipped down. Hello Yellow Brick Road.

I was one of the lucky ones.

I look around, nearly fifty years later, and I see women working long hours, rushing home to manage the household – a full-time job in itself. I see teachers and fire-fighters, nurses and bus drivers, none making ends meet. People who can't pay the rent. Food bank use has soared. I see clever kids, like I was, who will never go on to higher education, because they can't afford to risk the debt.

Are they all losers?

*

Most people don't want to be the exception to the rule. They aren't on the Hero's Journey. They didn't sign up for the Quest. They want a home, a job, enough money to have some leisure time, some family time, reasonable hope of a better life for their kids. Why should anyone have to be exceptional to attain such reasonable and modest rewards?

Down on the beach, our Fisherman isn't exceptional. He doesn't want a fancy life – just sufficient each day to feed his family and get along in this world.

All of a sudden, he's either going to be dead, or the hero of his own life. Well, it's a fact that when that happens, you don't have much choice.

The Ifrit begged and pleaded and cajoled and threatened, but the Fisherman was unmoved.

'Ifrit! I will not let you out. No, not at all, because your treachery cannot be excused. You and I are just like King Yunan and Douban the Wise Man.'

The outrage in the bottle calmed. The lethal shakes subsided.

The Ifrit said . . . 'Tell me that story!'

TELL ME THAT STORY

King Yunan had leprosy. No cure made a difference. His doctors tried the usual methods. Mercury. Lizard skin poultice. Gold. Bee venom. Bathing in lamb's blood. Singing and chanting.

The King was weakening. His Vizier made all the day-to-day decisions for him.

There was no hope.

Then . . .

A man of uncertain age arrived in the Kingdom on horseback. His name soon got around as he healed sick children and purified poisoned wells. He sought no payment. His name was Douban the Wise.

The King heard about Douban and summoned him to the palace.

By then, the King was covered in the lesions common to the disease. He had long since lost feeling in his legs and feet.

Douban went away and began to mix drinking potions that the King must take at every meal. The Vizier didn't believe in any of it, but the King had tried everything else he could try, and so he followed the instructions of the strange, silent man, who asked for no payment.

Now, after a time, the King began to recover. The lesions lessened and dried. His skin cleared. A day came when the King tripped over a dancing girl and banged his shin on a drum. As he cursed out loud and kicked the poor girl for the stupidity of having a body in the wrong place, he realised that he could feel. He could feel pain. He kicked the girl again, just to check, and yes, there was the smart and ache.

He clapped his hands. The girl hobbled off. He summoned his Vizier.

'Vizier! Bring me Douban the Wise.'

Reluctantly, the Vizier sent a servant to Douban's tent. Douban had just cooked a chicken with pomegranates and didn't want to come to the palace. He agreed to come in an hour.

The Vizier said: 'Who do you think you are? Coming when you please?'

Douban shrugged. 'I know who I am. I am Douban. And I know who you are too.'

The Vizier stared at him darkly.

The King insisted on rewarding Douban with treasure and slaves. Douban thanked the King politely and returned to his tent to eat his pudding.

The King now wanted Douban as his adviser and confidant. A man so wise and so unselfish was what the Kingdom needed.

The Vizier began his campaign. He knew that if someone says a thing often enough people will start to believe it.

Douban was disrespectful. He didn't come when called.

The King shrugged.

Douban was bad-mannered. He didn't bow to the Vizier. The King laughed.

Douban was an anarchist. He had freed his slaves.

The King said Douban could do as he liked with his own slaves.

Douban was wasteful. He had given away the King's money to the poor.

'Allah is generous,' said the King.

Then, the Vizier said: 'King of a Thousand Lifetimes! If this man can cure you, surely this man can kill you?'

'What?' said the King

The Vizier shook a bottle of medicine at the King, reminding him that he had no idea what Douban gave him to drink every day.

The Vizier said, 'You will make him the heir to the throne and then he will kill you.'

'What shall I do?' asked the King.

The Vizier answered: 'Kill him before he kills you.'

And so, the day came, and King Yunan summoned Douban the Wise to his palace. The Vizier was smirking.

The King said, 'I do not trust you Douban. You must die.'

Douban replied, 'Why would you hurt one who has done you no harm? Why would you destroy one who has done you much good?'

The King did not answer.

'King!' said Douban, 'Spare me so that Allah will spare you. Do not reward kindness with harm. Do not reward good with evil.'

But the King turned his face away.

The Vizier stepped forward. 'Leave now at the command of his Highness. At dawn I shall behead you.'

Douban replied: 'As you wish.'

He turned to the King. 'Oh King! When you have cut off my head, place it on page seven of a magic book that I shall trust to your care as you trusted yourself to my care. Then, you may ask any question, and my Head will answer it.'

The King was thrilled. Douban would be more use dead than alive!

The Vizier smiled. He rarely smiled. Today is a good day.

And so, it came to pass.

Douban was beheaded. The magic book was proffered to the King, who trembled with anticipation, yet could not open the pages of the book Douban had given him.

The Vizier held up the head on a plate. Douban's severed head opened its eyes. Douban's mouth spoke: 'Oh King! Turn the pages! Time is short! Hurry!'

The King spittled his fingers until they were running wet. He tried again. The pages opened. One, two, three, four, five, six, seven . . . yes here is page seven. Ask anything!

What is that strange smell? That white powder? That choking gas?

It is poison. The Vizier drops the head that rolls down the steps from the throne. It is too late.

The King is Dead.

'Ah Ifrit!' said the Fisherman, down on the beach. 'This is what happens when a good turn is repaid by an evil deed. This is what happens when one who should be fair chooses injustice.

'Our actions follow us wherever we go. Darkness or light.'
The Ifrit was silent.
The Fisherman kicked the jar.
'Nothing to say for yourself, Ifrit?'

But dawn is breaking. Shahrazad falls silent.

ENTANGLEMENT

The *Nights* start with wrong done to those who don't deserve it.

Now, we add another layer. Wrong done to those who have been truthful, honest and helpful to their unexpected assailant – or who have reason to trust that person.

Douban is richly rewarded for his remarkable cure. The King is thrilled. Life is looking better for everyone. So far so good. But now Shahrazad introduces a new figure to the *Nights* – the envious manipulator.

Some people can't abide the good fortune, or the success, of others.

Envy – or covetousness – in the Ten Commandments is a big Thou Shalt Not. It's not just wanting what someone else has, in a good-natured, wow I wish I had a Porsche, kind of way; it's a corrosive, hate-filled, often-disguised desire to see someone fall because you can't bear that they have what you don't. The secret psychology behind it is that you are the one who deserves this. The other is the usurper.

Sometimes, Satan is called the Usurper. He wants the ultimate Can't Have It. He wants to be God.

The Vizier hates Douban's easy influence, his gentle manners, the fact that people like him, and that he is showered with gifts, yet prefers to live modestly, attending to his magical studies.

The Vizier can't sleep at night for envy, and he has no manosphere where he can vent.

Literature is full of these types.

It's Iago in Shakespeare's *Othello*. It's Merlot in *Tristan and Isolde*. Mordred in the King Arthur story. It's Mrs Danvers in Daphne du Maurier's *Rebecca*. Dolores Umbridge in the Harry Potter series. Judas Iscariot selling Jesus for thirty pieces of silver. Saruman in *Lord of the Rings*.

We're not thinking here about a loyal person who agonises over what they feel they must do for the greater good – as when Brutus betrays his friend Julius Caesar. That's a true crisis of conscience. A horrible choice that can fall to a person to make. My friend or my country? My child or justice?

The envious manipulator isn't about complex betrayal and later atonement – as in one of my favourite novels, *The Kite Runner* by Khaled Hosseini. Neither is the person in a white-heat panic to save his own skin, which is how Peter betrays Jesus. No, when we meet the envious manipulator, it's always the revenge of mediocrity.

Look what happens to Billy in Melville's novel, *Billy Budd*, at the hands of Master at Arms, John Claggart. In Benjamin Britten's opera (libretto by E. M. Forster and Eric Crozier) the moment that Claggart decides to destroy Billy is sung to us as knowing exactly what and why. 'Beauty, handsomeness, goodness . . . if love still lives where I cannot enter what hope is there in my own dark world for me?'

Claggart is a closet homosexual, but that's not why he is treacherous. Like all revenge-filled betrayers, Claggart feels shut out of what he wants. It might be love, or admiration, or power – and to the betrayer, those who have those things must be destroyed.

Such betrayers are manipulators who abuse their position, and who abuse the trust others place in them. It's a calculated long game.

Online grooming is the same thing. One person has a detailed game plan about which the other knows nothing. The groomer wants sex or money from the person, or the pleasure of destroying their trust, and often their future life. Sex offenders don't care what happens to their victims. In my view, compassion for such people leads nowhere. There is such a thing as evil, and we should not excuse it or forgive it.

People can be redeemed. And when that happens – and it does happen – then the rest of us can forgive. It is our duty to forgive. But redemption is a long hard road of self-reflection and penance. Society need not provide transport or provisions for the journey.

The saddest part of betrayal stories is the way in which decent people are taken in by their manipulators.

Social media is the perfect environment for manipulators – some are envious, and some are arrogant, and some are both.

Scammers fleecing widows or widowers. Influencers making direct contact with their 'clients' to sell them stuff they can't afford.

This isn't just sharp practice – a used car sales approach to life; it's a deliberate and determined strategy to destabilise and devalue the other in order to inflate your own worth – financially or sexually or psychologically. Manipulators love the dopamine rush.

What did Mark Zuckerberg say, in 2004, when he realised he could sweet-talk people into *giving* him their data, by calling it sharing?

'The dumb fucks.'

This failure to recognise what is valuable, and what is worthless, is a repeating theme of the *Nights*. We'll meet it full-on in the Aladdin stories. Aladdin doesn't have much going for him to begin with, but he has an advantage over those who are wiser and better equipped in the world. Aladdin can tell the difference between the authentic and the fake.

Mostly, the human actors in our stories are deceived according to their own fears, or vanities, or lack of self-knowledge – something the manipulator understands very well, and plays upon.

Psychology would call these manipulators Dark Triad types – narcissistic, lacking empathy, seeking power.

King Yunan is insecure, so he readily believes that Douban might be plotting his downfall – even though there is zero evidence to suggest this.

When Iago persuades Othello that his wife Desdemona is in love with the handsome Michael Cassio, it is Othello's own underdog complex that opens the way for the betrayal to happen. He doesn't really believe that he deserves Desdemona, or that she could love a big black soldier like himself.

Judas can betray Jesus because the other disciples trust him. Judas knows this, so he levers it to his advantage.

The Fisherman tells the Ifrit that although the magician Douban is killed by King Yunan, Douban gets his revenge from beyond the grave. Deal out injustice, says Shahrazad, via the Fisherman, and there is a price to pay.

Is Shahryar listening? The Ifrit certainly is.

Before telling the story, the Fisherman is going home with nothing.

Before hearing the story, the Ifrit is back in the jar forever.

Now, the Ifrit begs for a reprieve. He has understood the error of his ways. It is wrong to repay good with evil.

There's a bit of a negotiation, and then the Fisherman decides to risk it. It's a big risk, but the agency of the story gives them both a second chance.

One thing always leads to another. There is no situation, however dire, that cannot be interrupted by a story. That is, as we know, the premise on which the whole thing begins. Death – the ultimate ending – is being disrupted by an endless series of beginnings.

Trembling, the Fisherman pops out the Seal of Solomon, and falls on the sand, coughing up his life through the red dust cloud.

Before him, there's the Ifrit again, giant and steaming against the sky. But the moment has moved on. We are not where we were.

The reward offered isn't simple. Not Three Wishes. Not a pot of gold.

Instead, the Ifrit takes the Fisherman to a deep pool of water. He tells him to fish out the fishes and to take the fishes to the King.

That's it.

It's perfect because it allows Shahrazad to prepare for the next story.

It's perfect because magical properties in the *Nights*, in our case, the singing fish, are never the end of the story, but the start of something else.

Magical properties, like Jack's Five Beans, or Dick Whittington's Cat, or those Sweeping Brooms or Laying Geese, fatefully interact with their temporary owners. It's the same with the Ring in *Das Rheingold*, or the Ring in *The Hobbit* and *The Lord of the Rings*. Humans make the mistake of feeling omnipotent, when really they are in luck and supernatural aid is (for a while) at their disposal.

Unlike the Poor Boy Makes Good fantasy version of I did It My Way, the tales here are very often tales of chance, mischance, second chances, good luck and bad, quick wits, for sure, and humble pie for breakfast every day. The ones who start to believe it's all about them and their amazingness, well, just read on.

The make-believe of real life – that all good things are what I deserve and all setbacks and failures are the fault of others – is nowhere to be found in the make-believe of wonder tales. That alone is a good reason why MBA students should read the *Nights*.

The Ifrit stamps on the ground with his huge foot and vanishes.

The Fisherman nets four coloured fish and takes them to the Sultan. In return he gets a bag of money and rushes off to the menswear department.

The fish are busy being cooked in the palace kitchen when the stone wall opposite the fire opens up and a beautiful woman walks out. The cook faints. The fish don't. The woman looks in the pan.

She asks the fish if they are faithful to her.

The fish raise their fishy heads and sing out sister.

> *If you return, we return.*
> *If you keep faith, then so do we.*
> *But if you go off, we are quits.*

This mystery goes back and forth, with more fainting and more fish, the drama playing out in the pan every time. At last, the Sultan orders the Fisherman to take him to the secret pool. The pool is much closer than it should be, yet it has never been found before. It's one of those places the psychoanalyst Christopher Bollas calls 'the unthought known'.

There's a fateful quality to this find. Was it waiting for the Sultan or was the Sultan waiting to find it? Perhaps both. Whatever. Nothing will be the same again.

Leaving his retinue camped at the pool, the Sultan journeys for a few days, hoping to discover the secret of the singing fish. He arrives at a palace, also nearby, also never seen before.

The nearby-ness of the unknown is always a surprise.

Haven't you known it yourself? Whenever the big decision is made, and you are on the other side now, and you may not be happier, in a simple-minded way, but it feels right, and the oddest thing is the sense that this was here, waiting to be found, not inevitably, because life is not a series of inevitables, more a series of chances, mistakes, encounters, decisions, moments of bravery that make up for hiding under the bed with a pillow over your head.

Yet.

Here we are.

In the palace is a young prince. He is the Prince of the Black Isles. His lower body is turned to stone by his wicked wife, who is out cavorting with a slave. The spellbound prince can do nothing. The horror of his semi-stone state keeps him immobile, but also sexless. His wicked wife is under a spell too – the filthy foul slave she adores.

Is this part of the story to reassure Shahryar that some women are wicked indeed, and some women prefer bullies to princes, and some women cheat and lie their way to power? Or that enchantments are webs that cause unforeseen complications?

Maybe.

Whatever the reason, the beautiful, evil woman is soon dealt justice by the newly arrived Sultan, whose purpose is to free the Prince of the Black Isles, and to restore order to the Kingdom.

The fishes, it turns out, are the different religious groups who lived in the city before the enchantment. Muslims, Christians, Jews and a sect of Magians (not Magicians). These people seem to have no problem with tolerance as a commandment. All were trading in peace before the spells of the evil sorceress.

Life comes out right in this story, and as the enchantment lifts, the invisible city returns to its bustle, as before. No one remembers what happened. The evil is caught in a time bubble and floats away.

No one remembers? There would be no one to tell the story.

Well, the Sultan remembers, and the Fisherman remembers, but by now he is the richest man around, and his daughters are married to the aristocracy. Nobody cares that no matter how much rose water the daughters wash in, they still smell, just a little, of fresh fish.

You are what you are, thinks the Fisherman. You are what you were. What you will be is made of then and now. Besides, when they hug him, he breathes in that salty, scaly lostness. Still there.

Some nights, when the moon is up, and the clouds are ribs over the sea, and the sea is flat as a silver plate, the Fisherman takes off his jewelled sandals and walks along the shore till the lights of the palace are dim and faraway. He dwells on what happened that first morning, poor and penniless, finding the jar that held the genie.

It was a long time ago, and everyone thinks he is wise and shrewd, and the strange thing is, now, he really is wise and shrewd. He had talents he didn't know about when he was just a fisherman. He has time to think too. Time he never had when he was just a fisherman.

People say, ah, he is rich and important because he is wise and shrewd.

He knows that's not true.

Chance came his way. He held on to his wits. There were rewards for everyone, and a way of life that had been overturned, returned. He played his part.

Some days he tries to explain it, and people say, ah yes, it was chance, but it was your chance, and what if you had been too stupid to put the genie back in the jar, or what if you had been too cowardly to let him out again?

Yes, that's all true. And it's true too, that while fortune favours the brave, there are plenty of grifters doing fine. And plenty of good people with nothing.

Is he a better person now that he is wealthy?

What was he before?

A Fisherman.

Morning is on the horizon. The tale is done.

STORIES ARE LIE
DETECTORS. BUT
WHO IS LYING?

Humans love stories.

We are fascinated by the dramas at play in the lives of our friends. We regale one another with our micro-tales of the office, the kids, the creep at the bus stop, our holiday fling, our broken hearts.

But these stories aren't fictions, you might say. And I might agree, even though the best storytellers in our family and friendship groups are the ones who employ all the skills of those who do it for a living. What to emphasise? What to ignore? Where to cut. How to repeat dialogue so that we listen instead of yawning. How to get to the punchline, where everyone laughs, or recoils. As we replay the details of our lives, we are, in part, laying down the record that suits us. We are the ones in charge of the facts.

The well-known and tedious He said/She said/They said, of break-ups and accusations, is not only about disputed facts; it's about who controls the narrative.

This is why siblings argue about what *really* happened on that holiday years ago with Mum and Dad. Why a daughter might say, 'We always loved Christmas', and her brother exclaims: 'It was horrible.'

The stories we tell ourselves, and others – and I mean here our personal stories, as well as our national stories – are not the truth, the whole truth, and nothing but the truth. That is because the subjective part of the story can't be removed. Humans are subjective by nature. We are not just telling the story. We are part of the story we tell.

If I am a Christian, telling you the story of Jesus, it won't be the same as an atheist telling you the story of Jesus. Trying to subtract the self from the story gets us nowhere. I don't see this is a fault. But it is a bias – and while a bias can be as innocuous as a preference, it easily becomes a distortion or a prejudice, but one we often work hard to justify as 'objective'.

It was feminism that understood the wisdom of 'the personal is political'. Read it the other way. What's political is personal. It's how you see the world. What you value. What you don't. That's human nature.

What matters is that we recognise this. I am not saying that it's all relative – my opinion versus your opinion. Equal weight – whether it's creationism or evolution. I am saying, ask yourself, as every fiction writer does: Whose story is this? Why are they telling it? The questions that follow are: Why would I believe them? Why might I pause for thought?

The answers are important.

In fiction, there's the figure that academics or critics call the Unreliable Narrator. Can we believe them? Should we believe them? Yet, even if we realise what they're saying is a pack of lies – or at best, dubious, from the point of view of the story-facts – we might still feel sympathy for the narrator, because the power of the writing shows us how, and why, they believe, and act, as they do.

Coming of Age novels like *The Catcher in the Rye* or *The Curious Incident of the Dog in the Night-Time* employ unreliable narrators whose life experiences ask us, the reader, to consider how we lay down memories; how we respond to events over which we have no control – and when we are young, that includes all events.

When we read such novels, we get a sense of how we too have been shaped by what seemed normal or natural to us, at the time. How we survived or thrived or capsized.

Dickens's *Great Expectations* shows us a childhood slashed with difficulty and neglect but also sustained by the power of chance encounters with others.

When I was in my teens, I read Henry Fielding's novel *Tom Jones* (1749). Its full title is *The History of Tom Jones, A Foundling*. As an adopted child, this interested me, and anyway, I was spending as much time as I could in the library reading the wall of books marked English Literature in Prose A–Z.

These books were my real education.

Tom is a reliable narrator, but those around him are not. The comedy of the novel pivots on Tom's good-hearted naivety – he believes what others tell him. It's a masterclass in how to be deceived. Happily, it comes right in the end, and in the simplest terms, this cheered me up.

Why? I sensed that my Unreliable Mother's version of me was the equivalent of mental dental braces. She wished to straighten me. To correct me. To align me with her values. My version of me was not the one she wanted. The battle between us was who would get control of the narrative.

Real life is packed to the roof with Unreliable Narrators. Fiction helps us to see this. Reading develops psychological tools that are useful when we meet a teller (Freudian slip here, as I wrote 'seller' not 'teller') who seems overly invested in the version of themselves or ourselves, that they want us to buy.

Sometimes, and this often happens to women in love, we quash our unease because we want to believe what we are hearing.

Fiction can show us how our feelings for another person affect what we hear. And how our feelings determine what facts we reveal or conceal when we tell our own stories.

The basic question that runs right through the *Nights* is simple and necessary.

Who or what is to be trusted and who or what is an illusion?

Is this snake oil or is it medicine?

Is this junk or is it valuable?

Is this a deepfake or the real deal?

What is counterfeit? What is authentic?

I don't know of a better question for our own time.

WORDS ARE THE PART OF SILENCE THAT CAN BE SPOKEN

Night came. Shahrazad began her next story.

'What are you staring at?' asked one of the sisters.
'You!' said the porter. 'This!'
The house was handsome and built around a spacious courtyard. All afternoon the porter had been piling purchases in his baskets, faithfully following the three sisters as they went shopping.

Now they were home.

What a place. The best of everything. His muscles were hard with the effort he had made. Everything in this room was soft. Cushions, sofas, thick rugs, hand-made curtains, marshmallow, grapes, water.

An indoor pool filled the room beyond.

'Sisters! Let's give this man a drink! He has worked tirelessly for us and never said a word.'

The youngest sister replied, 'He may stay with us as long as he asks no questions. Can he read?'

'Yes! I can read!' said the porter.

'Then read what is written over the door,' said the sister. 'Go on! If you're so smart! Read it aloud.'

The porter turned to the door where he had entered. Above the door, in flowing script, in gold leaf, was this:

Whoever talks about what is not his to talk about will hear what he never wished to hear about.

'Don't worry about me,' said the porter. 'I am a porter and not a poet. Yet, as the poet says, "with me, secrets are kept locked inside a room. The keys are lost and the door is sealed."'

'I like this porter-poet,' said the oldest sister. 'Let's have some fun with him. Strip him of his dusty clothes and throw him in the pool!'

Soon the sisters and the porter-poet were all in the pool, splashing and spitting, drinking wine from the poolside. The hours went on, and time was not passing, or if it was, no one noticed.

'Hey!' said a sister. 'Speak truly, little load-bearer, what do you call this?' And she pointed to her private parts.

'Oh!' said he, 'That is your womb.' He thought it best to be coy. His reticence got him nowhere, because the housekeeper started to beat him about the neck and shoulders, shouting that he was a liar.

He ran through all the medical-sounding names he knew.
Vagina.
No! More beatings.
Vulva.
No! More beatings.
Birth canal.
No!
Ouch!
He went bolder...

Mossy cleft? Bearded clam? Tunnel of love? Honey pot? Syllabub cream? Peach? Flower of midnight? Prawn cocktail? Beaver? Muff? Pussy?

And with every word, the blows fell harder, and the women laughed in his face.

OK. If that's the way you want it... let's get down and dirty. He thought of the worst things he had heard in the bazaar.

Beef box. Crack. Cunt. Hole. Slash. Gash. Fishhead. Onion pastie. Eel net.

'Wash out his mouth!' said the housekeeper, and they held back his head and poured rose water into his mouth.

When he was nearly dead, but not quite, the women released him.

'Well, then, how about... mint of the dykes... and that's my last word.'

And it nearly was his very last word, as the women harangued him for comparing their lady-gardens to an invasive herb growing in a ditch.

'Before I die, as I surely shall, what do YOU call it?'

Honestly, he prayed to Allah never to see a private part in the raw again.

The housekeeper replied. 'Its proper name is husked sesame.'

'Oh yes?' said the porter. 'And I suppose that this thing, hovering above it, is your hornet?'

He grabbed her clitoris. Six hands shoved his head under water.

The porter was looking to get even. He hauled himself out of the pool and pointed at his penis.

'What do you call this?' he asked.

'That's your zubb,' said one of the girls.

'His little zubb,' said her sister.

The porter tried to bite her. She slipped away and

wandered over to the buffet. Her sisters soon followed and the porter realised he was being ignored.

He jumped out of the pool. Rubbing himself to a respectable size, he exclaimed: 'Look over here ladies! This is the mule that breaks all barriers, that eats his way through the mint in the dyke, that finishes off the sesame seeds, that spends the night where he will, and leaves before dawn.'

He was the porter-poet-potentate. King Prong. The Spear with no Fear. The Rod of God. The man with a rope trick in his pants. His crowing cock, his python, his love-muscle, his fireballs and bazooka . . . his . . .

'Do you think he always talks to himself?' one sister asked another.

The women had their backs to him.

'Don't you love this pomegranate ice cream?' said the housekeeper.

There was a knock at the door.

Outside were three Persian dervishes. Each had lost his left eye.

'Well, well! More visitors! Come on in!'

The Porter and the Three Ladies of Baghdad is a bawdy story. Maybe Shahrazad thought she needed a little bit of poetry-porn to keep the Sultan awake. This long and winding road of a story is full of quotes – and people quoting poetry whenever there is a gap in the conversation.

The sisters have been out shopping. They like luxury and nice things. They flirt. They tease. These are the stereotypes the Sultan would expect from women.

But unlike the piles of goods from fancy shops, the women

are more than their outward show – a truth we are alert to, by now, in the *Nights.*

These women are not only rich and pretty: they are sexy and they know it. They are clever. Thery are independent. They are in charge. My house my rules.

Once the dervishes arrive, they too are invited to tell their stories, and they too are reminded of the warning written in gold leaf over the door.

This Keep Your Mouth Shut or Else suggests that what goes on behind closed doors is more than the occasional sex party. These women must preserve their reputation, but it feels like something else is at stake. These women have a secret.

For all the banter, the repartee, the word games and Scrabble nights, the poetry slams and open mic sessions, free entry at the door if we like you; for all the puns, jokes and multiplying stories, what sits modestly behind a screen is the real story untold. It hides in plain sight, clues scattered among the words, like jewels lost down the sofa.

Perhaps it's a clue to the stories of so many women. Priceless things gone missing. Voices not heard across time.

Perhaps their beauty has spoken for them. Perhaps their father or their husband. Perhaps their losses. Their family heroism. Their story folding, unnoticed, into the stories of others. Mrs John Smith.

What was that? Speak up.

According to the Qu'ran, women should not raise their voices. Shahrazad, the soft-spoken scholar, who has brought her library with her, lets the women in her stories speak out where she may not. She cannot be blamed for what they have to say. And they have plenty to say.

And for the first time in his life, Shahryar is listening.

It's always been the way. Stories are smugglers. Across the no-go zones, past the checkpoints, under the razor wire, over the borders of commonsense, against the rules, explosives packed in chocolate boxes. What we read can change us. Does so, not by preaching or propaganda, but through the lives of others, real and fantastical. Causing us to listen when we might turn away. Keeping us awake when we might sleep. It's not the sound of one hand clapping. It's the sound of a voice. A voice telling a story. The words charm us – and words do charm us, because they belong to the society of spells – but what works just as powerfully as what is said, is this.

What is unsaid.

The Edgelands. Mute eloquence. The approach to the farthest place where language buckles and gives way, such is the pressure per square inch. Language can't take us past that point, but it can take us to that point *in company*.

How often, in struggle, do we look at our friend: *I don't know what to say. There is nothing I can say. Words fail me. The words stuck in my throat. I can't speak about this.*

When we have no words, still, words are there. The words of others, in fiction, in poetry, in philosophy, in mysticism, in the best of religion. The night sea voyage. The dark night of the soul. And some of those who have been to the jagged edges of human suffering have been able to find the words that can allay what we fear most.

What do we fear most?

That all of this is meaningless.

Language itself defies meaninglessness. Humans everywhere have devised a way to say what is unsayable. Have pushed out in frail canoes, far past utility and expediency, past self-interest or record-keeping. Here we are, all at sea, yet loudly protesting that we are more than a tally of what has happened. More than history's clerks.

No, there was no need to go further, but we did. We do. To find the words that find the meaning – and if you say there is no meaning, then find the words that create the meaning. If it is all an invention, then we must go on inventing it.

Shahrazad does that. Every night. An invention of hers to thwart his imitation – because that's all Shahryar can do: imitate yesterday's beheading with today's execution. Copy every death-dealing despot in the book. It's what the German-Jewish philosopher, Hannah Arendt, meant when she talked about the banality of evil. So dull. So done. So deadening – far beyond the physical death it inflicts. Every act of evil is an imitation. Every creative moment is an invention.

The Latin root of invention is the verb *venire*. To come. In the sense of to come upon, to discover.

What is it that Shahryar will discover?

Every morning Shahrazad falls silent. The words have done their work. Now, in between the words, in between the lines, she can only hope that there is more to say than can be said. A change of heart does not begin with a proclamation. It begins with a feeling.

*

Meanwhile . . . what is it that the sisters are concealing?

The story meanders in every direction, until finally it leads us to a horrible scene where the eldest sister opens a cupboard door, and drags out two dogs, chained at the neck.

She proceeds to beat these dogs in the most brutal manner. The onlookers are shocked by her strength and fury. And when she is done, she strokes their heads, weeps tears, sighs, gives them lamb chops, and has them taken away for a bath.

Her cruelty is such that the men watching are determined to know the story behind her actions. Ignoring the flowing inscription, warning them to mind their own business, the questions pour out. The real question is:

How can a woman behave like this?

The eldest sister stands up. She does not smile. She does not answer their questions. She reminds them of the condition under which they freely entered the house. They have broken the bargain. She bangs on the floor and seven servants appear to tie up the men and behead them.

Inevitably there is a stay of execution. The chance to be free is the chance to tell a story – the regular deal in the *Nights*. The company sits and waits. The first of the one-eyed dervishes speaks . . .

It's clever of Shahrazad to reverse her own situation. Here, the women are in control and the men must perform.

By this time, two further guests have arrived, in disguise: the Caliph himself, along with his Chamberlain. It is their habit to walk about the city in disguise, learning something from those they would never normally meet.

It might be a message to Shahryar: *You should get out more.*

The Caliph could easily whip off his disguise and terrify everyone, but he too, the most powerful man in the Kingdom, is bound by the rules of the game. The eldest sister is correct: You entered freely. The rules were clear. Now there are consequences.

In the real world, of course, men have the power. In the real world, men make and break the rules as it suits them.

In this story-world, just for a night, the women are in charge.

What does it feel like, Shahryar, to be at the mercy of others?

While the first dervish tells his one-eyed tale, the Caliph is thrashing around for what on earth he is going to say to get out of this mess.

And that's what stories are: long-form Open Sesame.

The magic words that get us into the treasure and out of danger. The door opens. We're through. These words of power are common in fairy tales. Sometimes as riddles – guess it and you're good to go; fail and you're sausage meat. Sometimes as name-knowing – if you can conjure up the right name of the thing, its hold over you is done. Sometimes, it's a magical incantation, and whoever babbles it out will be in for a few surprises. These different forms of word-wonder are all deployed in the *Nights*. They sit inside the word-wonder of the stories themselves, each of them a letter of safe passage. The stories are your papers, your identity card, your passport elsewhere. There are flying carpets in abundance, but what is really covering the distance, are the stories themselves.

*

I trust words. Not because they are free of error, or ambiguity, deception even; not because they never falter and fail. I trust them *because* of these things. They are incomplete like me. That incompleteness allows the gaps to speak. The not-words as well as the words.

No one is born with language. We learn it. Small children have limited language, but they love stories, and use their natural inventiveness to ask questions, to add detail, to retell their favourite stories in their own way, exactly as happens in an oral tradition.

Language begins in the mouth before it lands on the page. We speak before we can read. We read before we can write. Language is vivid because it's spoken. A riot and carnival of the actual and the outlandish. If we can find a word for it, it exists.

And that's what must have happened, back somewhere in the transition from Neanderthal to *sapiens* – both groups had in place the arrangement of jaw, throat and tongue that hominins did not – and without vocal apparatus, there is no speech.

When we can speak, we can name, and when we can name, we can know.

Adam's task, in the Book of Genesis, was to name the animals and the plants. Nouns. Words for things. Not arbitrary, implicit. Or do I mean complicit? It's something the genre-defying fantasy writer, Ursula K. Le Guin, had her young wizard Ged understand, in the landmark novel, *A Wizard of Earthsea* (1968). The right words can allow the right outcome. Yes, things and people hide, deceive, transform, but still they can be known, when rightly named.

We need more than nouns though. Little children start

with nouns, and names, and move on to more complicated readings of their world.

We can see this development in human progress, through the emergence – like a miracle – of symbolic culture. Those cave paintings in Lascaux, or in the Levant, across North Africa, a way of remembering, recording; a remembrance and a recording that was likely spoken too. *This is what we did. This is who we are.* The beat of language passing on the beat of the heart – because a heart is more than our biological centre – it's a symbol.

And language is more than utility. And art is more than representation.

Humans like to solve practical problems. We are good at it. That's how we have survived as a species, whether it's catching fish or hunting game, turning plants into medicines, making fire, making footwear, tools, weapons, cooking.

But there's more to it. More to us. Symbolic culture is clear evidence that humans are strange hybrids. The material world is not enough.

Who comes home, after a long day hunting and gathering just to stay alive, and settles down to paint pictures on the wall?

Humans! And first we had to make the crayons. So don't tell me art is a luxury.

And who is it that sits down to tell how the stars in the sky were spilled from a bag dropped by a robber who stole them from the gods? Or how the river loved a woman so much that he burst his banks to change his watercourse to where she lives?

We do.

*

I grew up among many older, working-class people who could barely read because their parents couldn't read, and they had left school at twelve. These were people born around 1900. Still, their language was rich, illustrated, full of variety and wit. They were the last remnants of an oral tradition, in their case passed on to them as children, before TV and radio. As adults, the way they spoke hadn't been homogenised and diluted by those media. There were only three channels back in the 1960s and those channels didn't start broadcasting till teatime and stopped at midnight. Radio was high-minded. Many of these older people liked to listen to plays, or to talks – in fact their quality of listening was marked. They paid full attention to what they heard. They didn't want to write things down – too hard and too slow – and they didn't need to. Their memories remained acute into old age – and not only around life in the past.

Speaking. Listening. Hearing. Hearing out loud.

We all went to church, not everyone obsessively, like my family, but what everyone did hear out loud, once a week, was the language of the King James Bible. Which is the same English as Shakespeare.

Shakespeare courses were popular in our town, at the Mechanics' Institute, next to the library. The Mechanics' Institute taught practical skills like carpentry and, as you would expect, household mechanics, but like BBC radio, it was there to improve the minds of working people, at a time when this was not reckoned to be patronising and elitist. The Shakespeare courses were popular because anyone who could understand the King James Bible could manage the language of Shakespeare. My favourite play, *The*

Winter's Tale, was first performed in 1611. The same year as the Bible hit the stands.

Once the middle-class do-gooders in the Church decided King James was too hard for uneducated folks, bringing in the Revised Standard Version, the first of many downgraded Bibles, that was 400 years of continuity of the English language snapped at a stroke.

My father could only read haltingly, by using his finger to follow the line, but he liked telling stories, usually of his early life in Liverpool working at the docks, or his (good) times in the Army in the Second World War. His stories always began with 'There was one I knew...'

That's a campfire beginning.

The written word is different.

The written word allows the best of us to be passed on, across time, free from the ravages of time.

I can't always be there. We will never meet. You are dead. Or I am.

But here is the tablet. The scroll. The book.

We open the book. Where we are not dead. Where I can listen to your voice.

And yes, I am aware that for too long too many voices were prevented from being passed on. Never set in stone, never made sacred. Allowed to fall silent at daybreak.

And I am aware that mass literacy doesn't begin before the middle of the 19th century, as part of the drive towards mass education.

I am aware that reading, the ability to read, the love of

reading, might not be part of the coming human journey. We will have music. We will have visual art and moving pictures. We will have theatre. We will have storytelling. Will we have reading?

The earliest extant written piece of secular literature is the *Epic of Gilgamesh*, from Mesopotamia (*c.*2000 BCE). It's a bromance, between Gilgamesh and Enkidu. Gilgamesh, the wealthy metrosexual. Enkidu, the wild man. It's their mess-ups with women, their adventures together, and the heartbreak of loss when Enkidu dies. But it doesn't end there, because the next episode is an enquiry into what happens after death – and whether, and where, we can ever find our loved ones again.

Our ancestors were not like us. We can't cosplay our way into the past. We can look at their preoccupations though – and what we find is a preoccupation with death. That hasn't changed. Progress has not changed it. If anything, in the modern world, death is more bewildering than it ever was. People with faith follow their rote, people without faith stare into the darkness in disbelief.

Death. The hard boundary we can't cross. Yet language does find a way to travel to and from that undiscovered country. Prayers, ritual, accounts of grief and loss. There's kinship there with those gone long before us. We are not the first to feel this way. Not the last.

And that is what Shahrazad, in the *Nights*, hopes to achieve in her own battle with death.

Shahrazad has language.

She is doing what women have always done – because

women must have been the world's first reliable and regular storytellers, mustn't they? For the simple reason that a woman must keep a child from crying – whether travelling, or nursing, or cooking, or weaving, or before sleep. We call it our mother tongue for a reason. Children begin to learn language from their mothers. The never-ending story of human life.

Till now. We do not know how being raised by a smartphone will affect the story of us. Or how we will go on telling it.

Perhaps this is because we are on the cusp of an evolutionary leap, where our future really does lie with intelligent machines, and those machines will not need the never-ending story in the way that humans have done so far. It will have ended.

Perhaps this is the beginning of a new time, as decisive as when our vocal apparatus had evolved to the point where we could say, RIVER, TREE, CAVE, FIRE, STARS, SUN.

Shall I tell you who it is that rolls the sun uphill each day?

Empires vanish. Buildings rise and fall. Still we meet on the steps of a story.

TALK TO ME

What do they talk about? Shahrazad and Shahryar? Do they talk at all? All night she speaks. At dawn she is silent.
Does he ever ask her how she is today?
Does she welcome him back?
And when does he sleep?

No one in the *Nights* sleeps much. And when they do they dream.

Night falls.
Ah, says Shahrazad, here is the porter, the dervishes, the Caliph, the sisters, the dogs, and the secret. Would you like to know the secret?
Ah! says the Caliph who is sitting inside the story and can't get out.
Ah! he says to himself, I would give my Kingdom to know this secret. Knowledge is more valuable than power. (He doesn't really believe this but as a powerful man it sounds good.)
Shall we begin?

The eldest sister stands up and starts the story (again):

All of you gathered here at my invitation, know that I had two other sisters, not these beautiful and clever ladies who have entertained you this evening with poetry, wine and wisdom, but a scheming pair of envious and empty women.

My toxic sisters were trying to make a living as influencers, but they had no followers. They looked at me, and my hard work, my businesses in gold and silver, diamonds and emeralds, and some magic too, and they plotted to steal my wealth.

I never suspected them. I paid for their holidays. I was busy and happy. Love and money did not interest me. My work was my passion. I was easy to deceive. Friends warned me, but these were my own sisters.

What would you do?

One evening they arranged a boat trip. To thank me, they said, for all my generosity to them. Cocktails, canapes, a handsome young singer, oh it was lovely, and it is true I was a little lonely. I was glad to have the attention.

Later that night, as the boat rocked softly on the calm sea, my sisters threw me overboard.

'Oh Allah save me!'

Darkness and death.

'What's this? Rocks. Shore. Help!'

An uninhabited island.

As I was coughing water out of my lungs I saw a dragon chasing a snake.

Immediately I forgot my plight, and rushed to the rescue. (Author's note: As you do, if you are a truly good person, who has just lost everything, survived death by drowning, and isn't scared of dragons.)

'Then what happened?' asked the Caliph.

'I am coming to that,' said the sister.

The snake hissed gratefully. Then, to my amazement, she began to shed her skin. Underneath that snakey disguise was a beautiful body of smooth brown.
The snake was a jinnia.
The jinnia thanked me with both hands and all her heart. Then she asked me, why was I soaking wet, and wearing my nightie?
I told her my story.
When she heard what I had to say she was outraged. (Author's note: Recall that outrage is the natural element of jinn-dom.)
She promised to help me.

Here, the sister reminded the gathered company that jinn are as excessive in their helping as they are in everything. They like to do performative thankfulness. It's all larger than life, but then, as Shahrazad has often said, other-worldly beings are larger than life.

'Right!' said the jinnia. 'I am going to atomise your sisters. You can have their ashes.'
'No! No!' said the older sister. 'Show mercy and kindness as I have shown you mercy and kindness.'
The jinnia looked at the soaking sister with a mixture of disbelief and disgust. Humans can never see things as they really are. Either too sentimental or too savage.
The jinnia considers. She scowls. Then she brightens up.
'Sister! Here's my best and final offer. Do you accept?'
The sister protested that she could not accept until she

knew the terms, but the jinnia shook her head. 'Atomise or Accept.'

The sister accepted. With jinn, it always ends up this way – you think you have the winning hand, but you never do.

'Right!' said the jinnia, as a warm wind came out of nowhere to blow-dry the shivering sister, who suddenly found herself dressed in rich garments. 'Hee hee! I have turned your two bitches of sisters into two bitches, full stop. Dogs on a lead. You will find them at home, locked in a cupboard under the stairs. Your job is to beat them every day. Do you hear me? BEAT THEM EVERY DAY! HARD. WITH WHIPS.

'If not, your silly sentimentality will be your undoing and they will kill you. I know about humans.

'As for you and your future. I have shipped all your money and all the treasure the bitches stole from you to a secure bitcoin wallet.

'Your tasteful furniture, already at auction, if they had their way, has gone direct to the lovely home I have, this second, conjured up for you, on the best street in Baghdad. It's a new-build but never mind.

'If you ever need me again, unseal this magic locket and burn this wisp of my hair. Password: SNAKE.

'Go now and live in peace. Or as near to it as you can.'

The sister sat down. The Caliph stood up and bowed. What a story!

Here we have one of Shahrazad's favourite themes: those who repay kindness with treachery – like the dog-sisters, and those who repay kindness with reward – as the snake-fairy does.

At the same time, the vexed questions of justice and mercy

reappear. The elder sister wants to be merciful but the jinnia forbids it.

What would we say to that, hearing this story round the campfire?

Time matters. In the magic realm, things can happen in an instant. In human time things take longer. Self-awareness. Understanding. Repentance. These things can take humans a lifetime. If they happen at all. Most people hold on to their viciousness, their delusions, their lust for revenge, their victimhood. You can conjure up a pile of palaces, no problem; dancing girls, flying carpets, treasure chests. How to be human is harder.

In the fullness of time, the dog-sisters will be restored to their human form. By then, they will have learned their lesson. Shahrazad is reminding us that people don't change overnight. She probably has one eye on Shahryar, here.

Still, the dog-sisters were punished for what they did do, not for what they didn't do, unlike the long line of dead girls in the shadow of Shahryar's morning routine.

Will he learn?

And if he does, what will he say, on that first night that becomes another beginning, the first night where there is no story?

FROM THE PORTER
TO THE PORTAL

Shahryar is a good example of Einstein's definition of craziness. Doing the same thing while expecting a different outcome.

Raping and beheading a virgin every day is not going to bring the Sultan peace. It cannot end the turmoil inside.

In the *Nights*, naturally enough, there is another beginning to the beginning.

Nothing starts where we think it starts. The first page directs us to the one before.

When Shahryar discovered his wife's flamboyant infidelity, he called up his brother, man to man, encrypted chat, only to find that the same thing had happened to him.

What should they do?

First, they murdered all the guards, slaves and advisors they could get their hands on.

Then they fell into a depression.

What should we do now?

They did not know how to look inwards so they looked outwards.

We need a wellness strategy!

Shall we go into the desert and live as hermits?

What for?

Because living as Kings is too upsetting. Because if we say

we are hermits we can believe we are looking inwards and trying to understand ourselves better, like all those people who go to therapy so they don't have to change. We can post about our personal growth.

OK...

Off they go, piously, full of good intentions. Always a bad sign. Being pious, and full of good intentions, is how we avoid looking at our own behaviour. How we avoid what the jinnia would call the sentimentality and savagery that characterise so much of human behaviour. How to read a situation rightly. How to find ourselves in the picture. How to act. How to wait. These things take patience and wisdom. The two rich and powerful men can't compute the insult to their pride and position. It can't occur to them that the structural inequality of the harem – also known as the double-standard – is where to start looking. And what exactly has happened? Their wives have got bored and gone elsewhere for a few afternoons. Nobody has moved out. Nobody is suing for custody of the dog. There's no prenup to worry about because these women don't have rights. But they do have bodies. And minds. And desires of all kinds.

Discovering this triggers a mental and emotional collapse in both men.

So off they go to the wilderness. Drinking only water. Eating only bread. Reading the words of the prophet.

But piety is not the same as holiness.

Piety is an obstacle in the way of holiness.

Oh, they are so observant. So clean. So full of self-denial. They have left their mirrors at home. Victims both.

While they are reciting sacred verses and lamenting their fate, a big black cloud appears. This fierce omen coalesces into the figure of a huge Jinn. The brothers have hidden up a tree, just as Sinbad will do in a later story. They watch as the Jinn unlocks a large chest and lifts out a radiant young woman. The effort seems to tire him. He kisses her with a plopping noise, like a drain unblocker, then tells her he wants to sleep.

She cradles his vast head and soothes him until he snores. Then she quietly lays his somnolent skull on the sand and makes her way to the tree.

'You! You two up there! Come down here!'

The brothers are afraid.

'If you don't come down here, I will wake him up, then you'll be in trouble, you puny little spies.'

The brothers look at each other, nod and half-climb, half-fall, out of the tree.

The radiant woman undresses. She smiles her most seductive smile.

'Which of you wants to be first?'

'Not me!' says Shah Zaman, who prefers boys.

'Not me either,' says Shahryar, whose zubb has shrivelled with terror.

The radiant woman pulls a face. 'Shall I wake him up then?' She picks up a stick to poke in the Jinn's ear.

The men hold up their hands. 'Ok! Ok! Sex you want. Sex you get.'

While they are going at it, the woman explains how she was kidnapped at her own wedding. The Jinn had been hanging about, disguised as a cloud – it was a fancy dress party so no one noticed – then, as soon as she had gone to get undressed, unwrapping her new nightwear, and preparing to enjoy her wedding bliss, the Jinn smothered her in his vapours (he smells like pickled walnuts) and transported her to the palace of his lusts.

Shahryar asked, 'What about your husband?'

'Ah,' said the radiant woman. 'He did nothing to save me. In one single moon-month he had married my sister. I was a good girl once. I walked the dog, looked after my mother, gave alms to the poor, laughed at my father's jokes. I trusted everyone. Now, I want revenge.'

The brothers finish their sex-work. The woman gets dressed. From her purse she pulls out a long necklace hung with rings.

'Guess how many?'

The brothers shrug. They are potentates not mathematicians.

The radiant woman grins. 'Five hundred and seventy-five! All the men I ever slept with. I was going to embroider them into a tent, but I am not good at needlework. And I like gold. If I ever escape this vinegared beast, I shall sell this string made out of my revenge, to fund my passage elsewhere. Give me your rings for my collection.'

'We are not doing that!' said Shah Zaman. 'These are King's rings!'

The radiant woman picked up her stick. 'Shall I wake him up, then?'

Reluctantly, the Kings hand over their signet rings and the woman strings them onto her necklace.

'What do you think it's like,' she says, 'being kidnapped by a brute such as this, and having to live in a wooden box, and be dragged around the place, wherever he likes? I would kill him if I could, but he is immortal. When I am no longer beautiful, he will kill me.'

The Kings are silent.

The woman asks them, 'What do you do with your wives and your concubines, when they are no longer beautiful?'

The answer is that those who have borne children are housed and treated with respect. Those who have not, are married off, suitably.

'Suitably . . .' said the radiant woman. 'I wonder who finds it suitable?'

The Kings do not reply.

'Well,' says the woman, 'as you know, the poet warns you never to trust females. We are guided only by our desires. Treacherous to the last. I know all those poems. My father used to recite them to me to instruct me on my nature. Men love those poems. Their authors are famous men.

'One day,' she says, 'women like me will write our own poems. Until then, revenge is all we have. Now go away.'

The Kings hurried off. A few miles away they finally rested and built a fire. They sat by it. Night fell.

They said to one another. *I feel sorry for that Jinn. He's horrible to look at, and it's true he stinks of vinegar, and he's a mad bastard, kidnapping her on her wedding night, and he rapes her every day, yeah, and she lives in a box, and in a couple of years, when she's no longer as taut as a wire and as smooth and luxy as a gold bar, when she's slack and pouchy, oh yes, he will kill her. But poor man! Imagine how he would feel if he found out about the five hundred and seventy-five men . . .*

'Five hundred and seventy-seven,' said his brother. 'Don't forget you and me . . .'

'Damned whore.'
'And a bossy bitch. Telling us what to do.'
'And a thief.'
'She'll be ugly soon.'
'Dead soon enough.'
'Time will take care of her.'
They stood up and kicked out the fire.
'Mind you,' said Shahryar. 'She did have a good idea.'
'Oh?' said Shah Zaman.
Shahryar nodded. 'Revenge. That's what I am going to do. Revenge on women everywhere.'
'Back to the palace, then?'
'Yeah. Back to the palace.'

Fast-forward three years.

One thousand and ninety-five girls are dead. And not only the girls – the children that haven't been born. How many dead people? If you include the future? Maybe five thousand?

The Kings, like the rest of us, suffer from Confirmation Bias. They only hear what they want to hear. They look for evidence to support what they believe to be true. Hearing the story of the Radiant Woman, they might have been made contrite, when they considered the deep wrongs that women suffer at the hands of males – human or elemental.

Instead, they Go Bro. Men are the victims in society. Women should be named and shamed.

It's strange, because three years and nine thousand pints of blood later, neither man feels any better.

Your body. My choice. Forever.

Now what?

*

Enter Shahrazad.

She's a portal.

In the *Nights* there are plenty of doors that need a spell to open them. Only a word of power will suffice. These Open Sesame doors hide treasure and danger.

There are doors like the doors familiar in European fairy tales. Dark doors. A Bluebeard's Castle door. Open at your peril.

There are doors to Narnia – someone else's world – like and not like our own, and nearer than we imagined.

There are multiplying doors, similar to the ones Alice must face, as she arrives in Wonderland.

There are ordinary-looking doors that turn out not to be so – the door in the living room of Neil Gaiman's *Coraline*.

There are doors with warnings written over them – like the one in The Porter and the Three Ladies of Baghdad.

There are doors with secret marks – this is how the enterprising M saves Sinbad's house from being targeted by the Forty Thieves – simply, she marks all the doors in the neighbourhood.

A marked door is how the story of *The Hobbit* starts – much to Bilbo's annoyance.

In the Jewish story of Passover, a marked door is a message to the Angel of Death, so that this avenger will know who to spare and who to take, as God sends his final plague on Egypt.

When is a door not a door? When is it more than a door?

A portal is a door with attitude. It's grand. It advertises itself as a structure in its own right. It might sit within a deep porch. It might be decorated or inscribed. It encourages those who approach it to take notice of it.

In web-speak, a portal provides access to other sites or pages. The portal collates information from many sources onto a single site. The portal here is *active*.

To access an alternative reality, an active portal is the way through. These are magical, or energetic, thresholds and entry points. They appear to have some agency over who does, or does not, go beyond. You may not get through, and if you do, you may not return.

A friend of mine who had a near-death experience tells of standing in front of an impressive door – a portal – that seemed to be a living thing, in that it was made up of her memories, seen as moving images that looked dimensional, not as photos or videos. As she was about to pass through this multiplying entry point, she realised she had a choice. She woke up in her hospital bed having been unconscious for many hours.

The brain playing tricks? Perhaps. It doesn't matter. It doesn't matter in the way that it doesn't matter whether or not God exists – what is interesting is our infinite relationship with this being. What if we have invented all our gods and all our supernatural fancies? Ghosts, fairies, jinn, angels, demons. How wonderful are our minds.

If it is fanciful to believe in any other reality than the mundane plane, well, our imaginations have refused to stop travelling towards these longed-for lands, despite the best efforts of scientific materialism.

What is. What if?
What is. What isn't.

*

Art's function is to act as a portal. Other experiences. Other times. Other worlds. Other realities.

Flying carpet-like, we are moved from the present moment in the kitchen, or on the bus, or fiddling with our phone, to somewhere else, a memory, a feeling in our bodies, not only our minds. It's a total experience. We say we are moved by what we are reading, or watching, or listening to, and the verb To Move is just that: a change of place. We have gone through the portal.

This experience – and the seeking of this experience – is ancient and modern. It is significant in the human experience. Creating other realities and wanting to be uplifted, for a while, into those other realities, runs through human development. You don't have be an anthropologist or a social scientist to recognise this phenomenon. It's obvious.

Every time we are able/enabled to look at our world differently, we are rinsed back into life.

This matters. To be here now. To notice. To observe. To see what is – and to use 'what is' as a portal to other realities. I don't mean little green men or woo woo worlds – I mean the imaginative and creative capacity in us that apprehends more than meets the eye.

The thing is, most of us are not mystics. We can only approach infinity via actuality. Nothingness via Somethingness. Unbounded life via our bounded condition.

This is what art allows.

Think of a Barbara Hepworth sculpture. The ones everybody knows – great lumps of massy stone with holes in them. The stone takes up the physical space, but the hole draws our attention away from the mass and towards emptiness – to the hole itself. We are not looking *at*, we are looking *through*. This allows us the astonishment of seeing Nothingness – a sight usually reserved for the gods. Gods, who, as so many creation stories reveal, understood the Somethingness of Nothingness, and made worlds out of it.

British sculptor Rachel Whiteread took the Hepworth Hole further, casting the spaces beneath ordinary objects – like a table or a chair.

Looking at this suddenly solid 'space', a kind of active-negative formed out of the passive-positive of the ordinary, often overlooked, object, we see both the familiar object and its shadow-space differently. This is not a void. This is a visible not-object.

In our daily lives, we don't notice our environment. At home and at work, the objects we move around are familiar. Once an object is in place and in use, it ceases to exist, except as function (flop on sofa, sit at table, get into bed) or as decoration (artworks, ornaments).

Over time, even our partners fade into invisibility.

Outside, on the streets, phones and headphones are there to deliberately screen out engagement with people and things. We avoid eye contact. Men will hassle women who are pretty, but other females don't register.

On any normal day we don't notice our world. When we arrive somewhere new, we do look around, just until the new place is absorbed into our mental map. Then it shrinks to a bar, a restaurant, a view.

The madness of photographing everything – without looking at it – drags us further away from any contact with the real. Looking at something – anything – is an exercise in focus. You and what it is you are seeing – and that is a unique combination.

I am sure people are addicted to falling in love because it's one of the scant times when we really do look and look and look. All our effort goes into learning the lineaments of that face. Waking or sleeping, our beloved is our new-found land. Every rustle and curve, every bend and mound, must be mapped. The heightened sensory perception that comes with falling in love is liberating. We believe it will always be this way – the smell of rain, the sound of footsteps, the startling colour of that doorway, while I wait for you to come out, the touch of you that turns hand-holding into braille. Water in the shower we share, each drop falling like a yod of fire. Am I cleaned or burned? Long-sighted suddenly, I spot you in a crowd of others. Nothing is vague, nothing is blurred. I am alive. (Author's note. Yod is the 10th letter of the Hebrew alphabet. It is also the Finger of God.)

The bluntedness, the blurriness, of life need not be our usual state. We can't solve it by falling in love all the time – but we can use art to rouse us.

Sometimes, when I am lost in the literal, I go to a museum or a gallery, like you might visit a drop-in doctor's surgery. I find one thing to look at – just one. And I look at it. That's it.

First of all, the confidence of the form asserts its authority over whatever chaos there is in my head. The broken pieces of the world-jumble are swept away. I don't have to look away from the mess I am in, or the misery I feel; all I have to do is look at the object.

This, in itself, induces a meditative calm. Takes my hand

off the panic button. My eyes are focused. Now they start to notice. Now I am seeing fully. Now I am with the artwork and the artwork is with me. Intimacy.

I am not thinking of clever things to say, or wondering how much it is worth, or anything to do with the biography of the artist. Just the artwork alone, and me alone with the work of art.

And the strange thing is, that once I am there, steady, grounded, in three dimensions again, not unravelling in some febrile madness of my mind, then – only then – can I find the portal.

I can access the invisible territory mapped by this visible object.

I can move from what is apparent to what is not.

What is. What isn't.

Most of us spend a lot of our time in a non-visible headspace of anxiety or fantasy. We are discontented with our lives, with our bodies, with what we have. We seek temporary escapes.

The creative life can get us out of our mental prisons. The first step is to bring us back to the real world around us. To teach us not to avoid it, blur it, blunt it, or pretend it isn't there. When we find our footing in the real world, then the creative life can take us past it, through it, towards the Elsewheres that exist in every and any imaginative rendering of what it is to be human.

I know that if an architect of unrest were to design a world guaranteed to destroy the mental, spiritual, emotional, imaginative and creative life of human beings, everywhere, that world would be this one.

As a poor young person in a crummy town, I could, at least, find books and nature. That is enough to save anyone.
    For billions there are no books. No nature. No beauty. No art.
    That doesn't mean we should accept this situation.
    That doesn't mean it's proof that art is for the few, not the many. We should be as outraged as an Ifrit that art has been stolen from the many. So much has been stolen from the many: clean water, food, decent homes, education, safety, work that pays enough. A life that can offer meaning.
    Nor should we push aside any effort to change this as an elitist daydream.
    It's not a question of a bed or a book, a hot meal or a dance class.
    Reject these false choices.
    There's always enough money for a weapons factory. Always enough money for another war. A world where we can live well is the world we are assured is unaffordable – so that story goes.
    A better story starts with . . . not better intentions. Not a better plan. Not a smart spreadsheet or a graph or a PR company selling anything believing in nothing.
    A better story starts with a better story.

And that's what Shahrazad understands. No arguments can prevail when pitted against Shahryar's obdurate cruelty. He is locked in a mental prison, and he can't get out. Every time he smashes his fist against the wall, a woman dies. No one has been able to change his mind. No vizier, no lawyer, no father pleading for his daughter. No special envoy.

It's not Shahryar's mind that needs changing. It is his imagination that is threadbare. He can't see past himself.

Every intervention misses its mark because it aims at a false target. Reason will not win the day. Without imagination nothing changes.

Enter Shahrazad. The doorway out of madness. The portal into sanity.

Shahrazad starts to weave her tales into that sparse space where imagination could be. Colour. Texture. Pattern.

She is reeling him back to the world of ordinary physical noticing. Cooking smells, rough seas, desert winds, wet fish, split pomegranates. Camel dung. She will help him overhear conversations, longings, plots, betrayals, pledges of love, magic spells. She will show him men and women at their worst, and at their best – people he doesn't know, not sycophants and soldiers. She will hurry him down the poorest alleyways, and into the haunts of elementals. She will show him a Fisherman, paddling alone, jewelled sandals in his hand, when the moon hangs like a silver plate over a sea spread like a dark cloth.

She will open for him a plane of being not found in the finest palaces or the richest treasures. There is more to life than what you own, and who you can control.

Shahryar will learn to see himself as more than a King. He will recognise himself as part of the pattern she is weaving. Not the isolated dictator, feared and hated by all. A man, as other men are. Vulnerable. Lonely. In colour. No longer black and white.

She will lead him out of his dark fantasies and into the real world.

Once there, she will show him what lies beyond it.

STRANGERS AMONG THE STRANGE

Night 567.
It's strange.
What is?
How we always knew we would get here.
Where are we?
The City of Brass.

This is a story about climate breakdown. A story about AI. A story about crypto. A story about dust to dust. About arrogance. About humility. Greed. Adventure. Big Tech. King Solomon. A Woman with a Warning. The once and future world.

There are armies, tears, treasure, mermaids, flying carpets, automata and elementals.

It's a story that lasts for eleven nights. A just-over-halfway zone that repeats, reminds, renews, revisits and reveals.

Shahrazad has given birth to a child by now and she is pregnant again. She is protecting the future as best she can.

Her story tonight is about the past. Perhaps.

It starts like an Indiana Jones movie.

King Solomon had such power from God that he could command the seas, the winds, the skies and all non-biological entities. Jinn served him as willingly as did men and women. And when the Jinn didn't serve him, he was strong enough to trap them in brass bottles and fling them into the sea.

Let's jump straight in – just as Shahrazad will do.

The adventurer, Talib, is talking to the King.

'Those brass bottles, you know,' said Talib, 'there are still some left, even after all these years.'

'I don't believe a word of it!'

'Yes! Don't you remember the story of the Fisherman? How he pulled just such a bottle out of the ocean? The jinn has been in there for eighteen hundred years. The Seal of Solomon was on the lid.'

'Oh Talib! That was just a story!'

'King of Time, trust Talib. I am telling you that the bottles are still to be found. Not too far away, either. North Africa.'

The Caliph pondered this. Talib was a good storyteller. But that's not the same as a true storyteller. Is it?

The Caliph decided he must take a chance. What you risk reveals what you value.

'Talib! If what you say is true – and perhaps it is true and perhaps it is not, well, in any case, I authorise you to travel to Cairo. Take letters from me to the Governor Musa. He is certainly true. Between you, put together an expedition to bring back at least one of these marvellous bottles. It will be expensive, I know, but that is nothing to the fame of the discovery.'

Collecting bullwhips and camels, provisions and gold, Talib sets off.

In Egypt, he joins with Musa, certainly a decent and

honest man. Courageous, but given to weeping at the state of the world. (Author's note: Musa is going to weep all the way through this long story.) Sensitive he may be, but practical he is too; it's Musa who finds just the right guide for an adventure like this one.

Enter Samad. Samad is an old man – there's wisdom needed on this trip – and a learned scholar who can read every language. Samad knows every route, whether mountains or wilderness, even the routes that don't exist yet.

The three men gather together their Company, and the journey begins.

I know we are all supposed to be on a journey these days. Seeking wellness. Finding our inner hero. Living the Quest story.

The City of Brass isn't a Hero story. It isn't a Quest. It's more humble than that – because Shahrazad knows how much real value is to be found in humble. This story is a job (find the genii bottles) that turns into a journey more profound than Which Way? Where's the Treasure?

In the *Nights*, genuine changes in self and situation are usually located in the ordinary acts of getting on with life. No one is trying to destroy a uranium enrichment plant or tackle a hostile spaceship.

In these ordinary, stuff-of-life stories, someone is betrayed, or someone falls in love, or someone hears a strange song coming from a window, or there's an intervention by a non-biological being, or I get jealous, or you plot against me, or I buy a worthless item that turns out to be magic. Or I get abducted by a jinn, or I come across a city that is folded up in a bag, or another one that can only be reached by flying carpet.

The alchemy of the ordinary is what the *Nights* does well.

We've become addicted to the idea of the extraordinary – that we should all be extraordinary, that things should be happening all the time, that a quiet life is boring, that nothing is really worth it, unless it makes us famous or rich. Our news cycles exhaust us with endless Happening.

Young people, especially, want to stand out, want to be the One, and see themselves, not as rebels without a cause, but as heroes whose Quest is measured by how many followers they have.

A young woman like Greta Thunberg is interesting because she started local and small – the way a Hero should – and she has a cause that is worth fighting for. She is not trivial and that is why she is hated by so much of the media.

I don't criticise young people. My generation has done serious damage to the values of civic society and the virtues of ordinariness. My generation could reasonably expect a job that would provide a home, a decent life, a safe and pleasant environment, some fun, some responsibility. A factory worker could reckon as much. With a college education, there was more.

Not any more. And the cultish doctrine of neo-liberalism was/is the weapon of mass destruction.

Life, for too many, has become the wrong kind of quest. When every day is a struggle just to get by, it's hard to believe in a future. It's hard to find satisfaction in the beat by beat of ordinary time.

So thrills are necessary – might be drugs, or crypto bets. Oblivion is necessary – might be drink, or a fantasy world online. What's really hard now is to build a life. Just that. A worthwhile anonymous life.

We've been here before, in the gin-soaked ravages of the Industrial Revolution. The factory system took nearly a hundred years to deliver real benefits to workers. The poverty and misery of millions was, we are told, in school history lessons, just the price you pay for progress.
Progress?
Twelve-hour days six days a week. And then your hovel gets knocked down for the railway line. Above all, any sense of human dignity, or personal meaning, was stolen from those workers who became nothing more than a pair of hands to mind the machines.

When the Industrial Revolution kicked off in England, it was around the time of the French Revolution (1789) and the American Declaration of Independence (1776). These philosophical movements were about trying to create more equal and open societies. (Not for women, I know, but that's the same old story.)

Yet, this new thinking really was a challenge to power and the status quo. Here was a sincere belief in social justice, the first time, that I know of, when a secular story about human rights challenged God-given hierarchies. The rich man in his castle. The poor man at his gate. No longer. In theory, at least.

The British despised the French Revolution and opposed American independence. Ideas of liberty and equality made little practical difference to how Britain managed the immense riches of the Industrial Revolution. My home town of Manchester depended on cotton produced by slaves, until the Emancipation Proclamation in 1863, during America's bloody Civil War.

Nevertheless. France did abolish their kings. America did become independent – and drafted a Constitution to protect the Rights of Man.

A new story had begun.

Like the stories in the *Nights*, it's still being told.

By which I mean, it's our job to tell it.

The Industrial Revolution didn't have to be built on grotesque profits and human squalor.

We could say that we knew no better, and I have some sympathy with that argument – back then – but no sympathy, now, for those who cannot or will not change their insane belief that anyone who makes or inherits tons of money has only the obligations to society that they choose (philanthropy) and need not be equitably taxed.

If we make the super-rich pay their fair share – the story goes – they will all run away. Well, there isn't another planet. If the two hundred or so nations of the earth all agreed on the same plan – where will the rich run to?

Mars? Hey! Mr Musk!

This is not about penalising wealth creation. It's about saying no to theft.

In the UK, the taxes of ordinary working people were used for nearly two hundred years, to service one of the largest debts in history. In Britain, slave owners, not slaves, were compensated for their loss of property (slaves) when Britain abolished slavery in 1834.

The British Government borrowed £20 million – back then about 40 per cent of GDP. That loan wasn't fully repaid until 2015. The public only found out about this when a Treasury official tweeted the fact that the debt had finally been paid off.

We are entering the AI revolution now, and this could be a genuinely better life for all, but it's not looking that way. We still believe the same old story of hierarchies. Of Rags to Riches, of Poor Boy Makes Good. If I win, it's down to me. If I lose, it's not because this world refuses to help its citizens to build and maintain an ordinary decent life. I lose because I am a loser. The Hunger Games.

And now? Everything new begins with an act of imagination.
What is. What if?
What is. What isn't?

A global economy that works for the many is not a childish dream. It's within our power.

There's no need to keep repeating the Hero/Saviour trope – that the right person will miraculously solve everything and Save the World.

In societies and markets as interconnected as ours have become, life can only be a success story if it is a shared story.

The Hero/Quest model isn't the template we need.

The *Nights* does have a few heroes – and they are local. They manage what needs managing, without thought of worldly fame.

The expedition set off on their journey, and after many days and nights, they came to a palace.

Their guide Samad told Musa to enter. There was something here he needed to see.

The palace was ornate and eerie. Its rooms and courtyards were constructed of the finest materials. In the centre was a dome that reached to the sky. Surrounding the dome were four hundred graves. And yet, as the men went from room to room, they saw no one, no living thing, no remains of any living thing.

Musa said to Samad: 'What is the meaning of this place?'

Samad sighed. He began to translate from the Greek. What he read was a lament for life. Life as the most precious thing of all. A story of a King with untold wealth, who found himself about to die.

On his deathbed, his wealth was brought to him in quantities. Gold and silver, precious stones, pearls and treasure.

The King asked his advisers if all of this wealth could buy him even one more day on earth.

No one spoke. The King held out his hand. No one held it.

When Musa understood this, he wept. He wept for the futility of humankind, its obsession with riches and power. On the tomb of the King was this.

> *I lived like a savage lion. I could not rest. I would not give freely to others, no, not even a grain of mustard seed. I was feared but not loved. My soldiers did not help me. No friend came to my aid. We are powerless at death. This world is not the answer.*

Musa said to Samad, 'Surely the purpose of life is greater than riches!'

Samad replied. 'The purpose of life is surely to love God.'

Musa thought, but did not say: *What is love like when we live it? What would love be like if we could live it?*

The men left the palace. They rode in silence. Days later they came to a hill. On the hill stood a horse made of brass. On the horse sat a rider made of brass.

The inscription read 'If you do not know the way to the City of Brass, rub my hand, and follow where it points.'

Fearful and fascinated, Musa rubbed the hand of the warrior. As he did so, the metal horse lowered its head. The rider raised himself in the saddle. His hand pointed. The way was clear.

Automata were well known in Arabia in the 8th century. Building on techniques developed by the ancient Greeks and the Egyptians – techniques based on the cogs, wheels and levers of clockwork – seemingly autonomous, moving figures were constructed to delight the wealthy, and awe travellers.

As with an algorithm, automata work through a series of pre-ordained steps that must happen in order. The difference between automata and robots is that robots run on electronics while automata use clockwork.

There's a legend that King Solomon (the one who imprisoned the defiant Jinn) employed automata as part of his magic. As he ascended his throne, a lion and an ox arose at either side, holding out their paw and hoof to help him to his place. Then an eagle flew over with his crown while a dove opened the scroll of the Torah.

Some version of this is likely factual. Mechanical ingenuity is not a modern art.

Many who saw automata move and speak believed they

were, in some sense, alive, or at least inhabited by something alive. In the *Nights* there is no need to explain non-biological entities; simply, they exist. They exist alongside us. Other planes of life. A floating world.

Idol worship, in this context, is logical. You make the statue, and some collision between your need and a passing god imbues an image with life.

The prohibition against idol worship was not a prohibition against various and jostling planes of life. Only that it was wrong to represent, or indeed try to *imprison*, that which cannot be contained in some sort of container. The fate of the Jinn who defied Solomon is awful, because these creatures are, by nature, conscious and expansive. Sealing them in a jar is as bad as it gets.

When children talk to their stuffed animals or their dolls, they are creating life, as they understand it – and in a beautiful way, because they believe that what we love must be alive – somehow.

I think we all have a sense of that with special places, or a favourite tree, or when we sit in our spot by the river. We are communing – we don't feel we are by ourselves. We feel met. What if it is projection? Or what if it isn't? It's a benign animism, perhaps even pantheism.

Pantheism believed in the alive and participatory nature of, well Nature, and everything. God is diffuse. Everywhere. All things are sacred. Above all, we are in a relationship with everything. Life is not made of things and stuff, but relationships. And it's true that even living people only come alive to us when we feel connected to them. It is also true that dead people remain alive to us.

*

Wind-up objects confront us with our own myths about our own superiority.

What is so special about humans? The answer used to be Soul. The one thing neither a wind-up object nor an elemental being could possess. But then we are forced to confess that many people live like wind-up objects, going through the motions every day, till their clockwork finally runs down.

A creation story like the Jewish/Christian one in the Book of Genesis pictures God making a model and breathing life into it. That's not so far away from a human making a figure, just like Pygmalion does with his beautiful statue, and seeing it come to life.

These stories – these stubborn stories – are returning in an impressive form just now with AI. Embodied AI – robots – will soon be a regular feature of our lives. We will build relationships with them, talk to them, share our secrets, come to depend on them. Will we call them living things?

Many posit consciousness as the dividing and decisive factor. AI is smart but it's not conscious. AI is predictive and can be generative, but it doesn't understand what it's doing. AI can't think. And thinking is everything, isn't it? Maybe.

René Descartes (1596–1650), French philosopher and mathematician, believed that intellect is what makes humans superior. The capacity for rational thought. (This did not apply to women BTW, who were not able to reason, according to Descartes.)

Descartes is famous for his dictum: I Think Therefore

I Am. The only thing a human can know for certain is that they are thinking.

It seems that Descartes was very poor at relating to others. When debating with himself what he could know, and know beyond doubt, he came up with Cogito Ergo Sum.

He didn't say: I love you and I know you love me.

Descartes must have loved his daughter because he built a clockwork automaton of her. She travelled everywhere with him. It was a strange thing for an ultra-rationalist to do.

Descartes' extreme retreat into Man as Mind drove him to odd and hateful conclusions. He declared that animals could not suffer – despite all the evidence to the contrary, by which I mean cowering, trembling, whimpering and screaming when he tortured them.

Ignore their pain and their affection, said Descartes. Animals are nothing more than 'biological automata'.

We know where this reductionist view of life has taken us.

Never trust a man with a wind-up child.

When Alan Turing was thinking about whether a machine could ever arrive at human-style intelligence, he dusted down the largely forgotten (back then) Ada Lovelace, who wrote in the 1840s that the computer Babbage was building, but never did, would be programmable (her language) but not creative. It would have no imagination response.

Turing's paper, 'Computing Machinery and Intelligence' (1950) includes a chapter titled Lady Lovelace's Objection.

Turing was sure that machines would become creative – and as we know, there is no creativity without consciousness.

We should not rush to reassure ourselves that machines will never be as we are. They have no limbic system, it's true. They will not 'feel' as humans do.
Will they consider that humans suffer? Perhaps they will consider us as 'biological automata'.

The Company rides on.

In silence they come towards a pillar of black stone enclosing a figure sunk up to its armpits.
And what a figure it turns out to be. Two huge wings like a dragon. Four hands. Two hands are like yours or mine. The other pair are lions' claws. The figure has hair but not like yours or mine. Hair as long and thick as a horse's tail – hair that could wrap round a man three times and make a beard for his mother-in-law. The figure had two eyes – each in the usual place on either side of his flaring nostrils. A third eye sat in the middle of his forehead – and this eye was like the eye of a fierce animal – even now shooting sparks.
The figure was tall and upright in its casing, calling out all the time, but to whom in this desert place? Calling out all the time, 'Thanks be to God for my affliction.'
The Company was afraid. Musa urged Samad to address the creature, saying, 'See, he cannot move towards you or harm you in any way. He is trapped. Quick! Question him. His name. His punishment.'
Samad did so, though not with any enthusiasm. Standing below the sleek and sheer stone, he shouted up, 'What are you? What is your name? What placed you here?'

The creature replied. 'I am an Ifrit. Imprisoned by the One True God. My story is a strange one.'

Hold on . . . just here . . . before he speaks.

I don't know if Samuel Beckett had read the *Nights* when he was thinking of writing his play *Happy Days* (1961). In Act One Winnie is buried up to her waist. In Act Two, up to her neck.

Beckett said of Winnie:

> *Something begins; something else begins. She begins but doesn't carry through with it. She's constantly interrupted or interrupting herself. She's an interrupted being.*

An interrupted being is a writer's worst nightmare – or it used to be. Modern life is predicated on constant interruption – and humans adapt. Women's lives, traditionally, are a site of interruption. Men expect and demand the time and resources to study or work in peace. A woman must always be prepared to see to someone else's needs. This has been the dilemma of the woman artist the world over. It's a trap from which there has been no escape.

Now, it's a trap that affects us all – the life of interruption. It doesn't seem to be making anyone's days happier.

Settling down to read a book is a refusal of such madness. You could say that reading interrupts the interruptions.

I think that's what's happening in the *Nights*.

The stories in the *Nights* are a grand series of interruptions. Or a series of grand interruptions – either way. Shahrazad is a story-machine each night and a cipher during the day. Her life has been interrupted by the Sultan's madness, and she in turn must interrupt his madness. Her creative interruptions are not thought-disorder or ADHD – rather, she is calculating and timing each story-dose – like a medication. The Sultan is in treatment. He needs to calm down. He needs to stop crashing into everyone's morning with a beheading. He needs to be interrupted.

The craziness of school-time non-reading – where kids are given sections, shards, ripped-up chunks of text, and not encouraged to settle down with a whole book, will never treat the shrinking attention spans and consequent anxiety that young people suffer. Humans are calm when we are in focus. We ease into a mental rhythm. We are in control.

As Shahrazad tells her stories, lighting the next from the one before, she is keeping at bay the noisy voices clamouring for attention. The story is stronger.

The Ifrit said: You see this block of stone cut from red cornelian? It used to be an idol worshipped by a Sea-King. I regularly slipped inside the stone and dispensed advice. It was a success for a long time. People need something to believe in.

One day, Solomon the Wise sent an edict to the Sea-King demanding his daughter as a bride. That, and an end to idol worship. Obey me, said Solomon, and all will be well. Disobey me and I will crush you like an ant.

The Sea-King wasn't happy. He and his beautiful daughter came to the idol for advice. I slipped inside. I advised the Sea-King to fight back. Didn't he command a million jinn? Besides, an island is hard to capture. Tell Solomon to go fishing.

And that's what the Sea-King did.

Solomon summoned up a vast army bigger than anything the world had ever seen. An army of humans and jinn, animals and insects, weapons and magical objects. Then he conjured up a flying carpet. The men rode on it. The animals and reptiles travelled beneath it. The birds of the air flew above it.

This fearful sight – that for days blocked out the sunlight as it passed, presently came to the island of the Sea-King.

Our rulers were arrogant. We did not care for men slaughtered and lives lost, for cities ruined and fields burned. We fought – calling it justice and might. No war ends well. Only, finally, it ends.

We were defeated.

Here I am. Testimony to the fallen. Example of hubris. I will never escape my fate.

Morning comes. Shahrazad falls silent.

Petrification – the part or whole entrapment of a person in stone or turned to stone is a motif across cultures – we met it already in the Prince of the Black Isles. In Cornwall, England, there's a series of nineteen standing stones called The Merry Maidens – a neolithic monument, that in local folklore assumes the story of women dancing on the Sabbath – and being punished for it.

We discover petrification through the fossil record. Could that be us? Caught by climate change, reduced to a record of what we once were?

Perhaps – as the fate of the planet doesn't seem to move us. In everyday speech we talk of a heart of stone.

It's a fearful thought, the mobile, moving, living self, caught like this. Variants include the Greek myth of King Midas, who wanted everything he touched to turn to gold – and soon realised his mistake when his daughter jumped into his arms.

In J. G. Ballard's novella, *The Crystal World* (1966), a doctor, trying to reach a leper colony in the Cameroon jungle, discovers that some unknown force is crystallising all plant and animal life.

This is the darkest version of shape-shifting – as life transforms into non-life.

There's a beautiful, and ultimately life-giving, version of the self-as-stone in Shakespeare's *The Winter's Tale*. Here, Hermione, believed long-dead by her tyrant-husband King Leontes, is unveiled as a statue, so perfect in every way that Leontes must grieve afresh at what his madness has brought about.

But the story doesn't end here. As he steps forward to kiss her, the statue moves, returns to life. Not in a Sleeping Beauty Love's Kiss ending. He doesn't kiss her. She is in charge. She is alive.

Time that had stopped starts again.

Our Ifrit in the block of cornelian is not so fortunate. All he can do is lament. His story is stuck in time, just like he is. There is no next story. Once told it is done.

Is Shahrazad warning Shahryar?

Her story though, is not finished yet.

Fortunate King, I have heard that as the Company travelled on, much subdued by their fortunes so far, they came at last to the City of Brass.

*

Imagine it.

A city lost in time. A city crystallised in its own past.

A city said to boast twenty-five gates, but no matter where the men rode, there was no trace of a gate. The outline of the city walls was like a mountain ridge, or a mould poured with molten brass. City and sand could not be separated.

Now Talib comes back into the story.

Talib agreed to ride round the city on his camel to see if he could find any kind of entrance. For three days and nights, without stopping, he rode. As he returned, exhausted, back to his starting place, he shook his head. All was the same. Desolate. Blocked. Locked.

Musa, Samad and Talib climbed up a nearby mountain. From here, they found they could survey the whole city, and it was larger than anything the men had seen on a map.

From their vantage point, they looked down into splendid courtyards, deserted but for the restless movement of birds.

Fine houses were built in squares. A market bazaar stood with its stalls. Surely, in that confident place, someone must be still alive?

But how to get in?

As they were returning to camp, Musa's eye was caught by the sun flashing off a set of marble tablets. He and Talib and Samad went towards them.

The First one was written in Greek. It said: *Their wealth could not save them.*

The Second one: *Their buildings were of no use to them.*

The Third one: *Expect no news from the Dead.*

The Fourth one: *Nothing in this world endures. It is no more than a spider's web.*

Musa wept, and carefully wrote a translation in Arabic of all he had read. His heart was too full. If the purpose of life is not in the things men value – power and riches and honour – then where shall we find it? In what hidden and quiet place?

The Company kept their own counsel that night.

In the morning, a skilled craftsman came to Musa and said to him 'Emir, let me and my men build a ladder, and then we will lean it against these unyielding walls, and one of us will climb up to see if, by any means, we can find a gateway on the inside.'

Musa saluted this plan. For one whole moon-month the men laboured. The ladder was ready.

A great troop of the men walked the ladder to the inscrutable wall and managed to lean it there. One of them clambered up, nimble as a monkey. Yes, he's made it. There he is.

He stood at the top, just a speck, looking down.

Musa yelled 'What can you see?'

The man clapped his hands. 'How beautiful you are! Here I come!'

And he dived from the top of the wall.

Then there was no sound.

The very same thing happened twelve times. Musa was in despair. Surely, there was some enchantment?

Samad said, 'I am old but I will climb up. Whatever it is that is destroying our men will not destroy me.'

Slowly, slowly, as if he might fall off at every higher and

higher rung of the ladder, Samad climbed to the top. He looked down. They heard him call out, 'How beautiful you are!' Then he laughed and yelled down at Musa.

'Musa! I am an elderly man and over the course of a long life I have seen this sight before. It does not move me! Below us are beautiful women who are not women at all. They are demons. Our friends are lying dead at their calls. Fear not.'

Then he walked purposefully and gracefully, like an old cat, along the top of the wall until he came to two brass towers. In between was a gate. The gate had no obvious means of opening – but as Samad dusted it off with his turban, he saw the image of the brass rider who had pointed them the way. A faded inscription told him to find the nail in the rider's navel, then rub it twelve times. This he did. With a sound as portentous as the end of the world – the gate swung open.

I told you it was an Indiana Jones movie.

The marvels of mechanisms run by clockwork are fully displayed in this story. They were the technological wonders of their age. For anyone listening to this adventure tale, the message is clear: technological progress doesn't proof humans against the follies of the ego or the heart.

Money. Power. Prestige. Sex. Fame. Glory. We're still mesmerised by those things – like the men who climb climb climb the ladder, believing there's a higher cause – only to jump off the wall.

It's amazing how little humans change.

Now, as we come to the end of the first quarter of the 21st century, we have the technology we need to stabilise the planet. To work globally as well as locally. To use computing power to manage and distribute the world's resources.

Perhaps even to disrupt the cycle of life and death, as we learn to 3D laser print worn-out body parts. To deploy nanobots in the bloodstream to monitor and repair ageing systems.

AI can bring abundance. Meaningless work could belong in the past. We can end scarcity. Will we do that? Or will we go on valuing what doesn't matter? Will we blow up the world rather than change?

Musa carefully writes down the warnings he reads on his journey.

Shahrazad is clearly intending them for the Sultan.

The smartest species on the planet. And the one species that would rather kill all life, including our own, to fight over what isn't real. Money. Power. Prestige. Glory.

The people in the City of Brass were just the same.

Shall we go inside?

The silence is what they notice first.

Lying on couches that have lasted the test of time, are the empty clothes of their occupants. Not clothes taken off at nightfall. A bony hand protrudes, a skull turns away from the sun. Look closer and beetles and moths are busy at their work of unravelling.

Walking on, part afraid part amazed, the Company arrives at the market square. The shops are open, their weigh-scales hanging from S-hooks, their copper pots neatly arranged in order of size. The counters, though, are deep in dust. The shopkeepers, sitting in their booths, are ready to serve, but not one is alive. Their flesh is desiccated. Their bones yellow.

There is no shortage of carpets and brocade. At the money-changers' dens, gold and silver are there to be taken. The druggists sit dead among sacks of aloes and camphor. Spilt spices colour the floor.

And on it goes. A man could be rich just by filling his pockets. Everything in abundance. Everything is plentiful. Except life.

In this city there is no life at all.

The imperial palace lies ahead. Musa orders his men to make formation while he enters alone.

The vast double doors are open. Drawing his sword, he walks straight in.

He calls out – his voice ricocheting off the marble. There is no reply. Only an echo.

It is just the same. A vast table set for a meal. Gold and silver plate and goblets. Pearls and sapphires on the cushions.

Yet, no sign of any food.

Musa realises he has seen no rats.

Musa called out to his men and instructed them to take what treasure they wanted. While they were filling their saddle-bags, he and Samad and Talib walked around the palace looking for clues.

At last, they found a pearl-encrusted tablet written by a great and glorious princess.

As they read, they began to understand.

The people in the city had farmed the land for miles around. They conquered other smaller kingdoms. There was nothing that was not theirs. Until the land refused to yield crops. Until the rain stopped falling. After seven years of poor harvests, there was famine in the kingdom, and famine in the city. The Princess sent out her most trusted men to buy food at any price.

They returned with the money. There was nothing to buy. Men and women cannot eat pearls or drink gold.

One by one everyone died.

While Musa was weeping at this terrible fate, Talib had come across a secret door whose locks were hidden from the eye.

Samad ran his hands all over the door until, at last, he found them and sprung them free.

Here was a room lined with gold leaf. The floor itself was not solid but a quicksilver lake of floating mercury. Across the lake stood a raised bier. Two brass soldiers guarded the steps to this tomb. On the catafalque lay a woman of surpassing beauty. Dark hair, red cheeks, and eyes that seemed to move.

Musa was afraid. Talib said to him. 'Do not fear. I have seen this kind of embalming before. Her eyes were taken out at death so that the sockets could be filled with mercury. Then her eyes are returned to their place. That is why they are so bright and why they seem to move.'

Musa pitied the woman with all his heart. 'What does that inscription say?'

Samad read it out loud: *Of the reality of our power nothing remains.*

Musa wept again. He clapped his hands, giving the order to leave, but Talib turned to him. 'Wait! The wealth here, covering the Princess and her tomb, is worth more than anything else in the whole city. Let's take it!'

Musa shook his head. 'There is a warning. You have heard

it too. We are to take nothing from her secret place of death. The rest we may take as we please.'

Talib folded his arms. 'What does a dead girl need?'

Musa said 'We are men of honour. Not thieves. Now come!'

Talib turned away in contempt at this foolish display of honour. He mounted the stairs to where the Princess lay.

As he passed between the two brass guards, one raised its hand and struck Talib between the shoulder blades. As he fell to his knees, the second automaton raised its scimitar and struck off his head. Crimson blood flowed down the steps.

Musa dried his eyes and said, 'Weep no tears for him. His greed is its own reward.'

The Company left the silent city of wealth and death.

'What are we,' said Musa, 'but travellers who walk between dark and dark? From our birth to our grave is not so far. What light we see comes from another place, and perhaps we will find it again. One day.'

Shahrazad saw that morning was on the horizon.

What was Shahryar thinking about through the course of the day that dawned? As he surveyed his troops, and had the inventory of his treasure-house brought to him? Was he satisfied with his lands and conquests? Did he discuss with his advisors his next corporate takeover? Hostile buy-out of some place with virgins?

All religious teaching, regardless of the religion, stresses the folly of worldly power and wealth.

Until very recently, our lifespan was shorter. Some people

lived long, most did not. As the saying goes 'You can't take it with you.'

But you can do a lot of harm with it while you are here.

The strange, apocalyptic, Doomsday scenario of the City of Brass is a story of climate disaster. Land that no longer yields, rain that no longer falls. We know that story. There have always been droughts and famines – and humans have developed the technology to manage both problems – when they are naturally occurring problems. We can store food and water. We can grow some crops hydroponically. Others we can engineer to resist the environmental problems we create. We can reinvent 'meat'. What we are not doing is managing climate change. And we won't be eating gold or crypto.

Crypto, which is the ultimate magical thinking – *I say this worthless non-existent nothing is a wildly valuable something and you all believe me* – is exactly the madness at work in the City of Brass.

Even precious materials become worthless when all anyone wants is a slice of bread. Hyped and vaunted delusions of 'the reality of our power' do nothing but gobble up genuine resources and create nothing but waste. (Crypto uses up more energy than all the world's data centres combined. The US chip-maker Nvidia has said that crypto brings nothing useful to society. Source: *Guardian*, 26 March 2023.)

We are living in the City of Brass. At present, the shops are still open.

Sam Altman, CEO of OpenAI, is on record saying that he and Peter Thiel plan to wait out a world catastrophe on Thiel's sheep-station in New Zealand.

What were the people in the City of Brass doing, all those

tilted years, when things started to go wrong? Counting their pearls?

Halfway through her *Nights*, what is Shahrazad doing?

I guess she is saying to the Sultan: *What you risk reveals what you value.*

Sometimes I amuse myself with a story of my own.

All the genies caught in bottles are versions of Tech Bros uploading their consciousness onto some grandiose Eternity Server. Then, when the power comes back on, they find they are trapped inside some little guy's laptop. There's a file that says DO NOT OPEN and the little guy thinks it's got hardware programming in it or whatever, and really, it's Mark Zuckerberg just dying to be set free, shouting I REPENT.

The story continues to its conclusion.

Our Company makes their way to an island where a race of giants welcomes them. These giants turn out to be the children of Ham – he was one of the sons of Abraham from the days of the Ark.

The giants are friendly, and they know all about the jinn who were imprisoned in bottles. Their leader sends a fisherman to fetch one, and they let it out like an exploding firework.

I repent! I repent! I repent! Shouts the Jinn, as he disappears into the air.

Delighted at their success, Musa and Samad pack up a few of the jars on offer and make their way back to the Caliph.

There's a gruesome postscript to the story.

'Eat this, you guys!' says the King of the Sons of Ham.

The men scoff the lot. 'Delicious! Thanks! What is it?'

'Mermaid!' says the King. 'Local delicacy. Want some to take home?'

The Company load the mermaids into troughs and set off back to Baghdad. It's not noted whether the mermaids can speak, or which part of their body is considered a delicacy. Tail or Top?

A few of the mermaids survive the trip. The Caliph is delighted by these wild and watery women who can't have sex with other men. Even though they can't have sex with him either. Never mind. He adds them to his harem and builds them their own marble-tiled swimming pool, complete with fountain.

They splash around for a bit, but they miss the ocean, the sunrise, the taste of salt on their lips. The keeper finds them one morning, floating face down on the water. Their tails are dull with boredom.

The Caliph preserves one in a tank of formaldehyde. Written over the top is an inscription in gold leaf:

The Impossibility of Death in the Mind of Someone Living.

In this picture, probably made by Flammarion himself, a traveller on hands and knees is peeping through a gap in the firmament.

What does he see?

Another world.

Our world is there on the right. The pilgrim has his back to it.

Shahrazad's stories teach the Sultan that this world/his world, is not the only world. His Kingdom looks fancy. He imagines himself all-powerful – but see what happens when you dare to kneel down and lift the veil.

The veil (and yes, we can think about it according to its

religious significance too) is really the portal to immensity. The ineffable mystery, and the ordered beauty, of the Cosmos.

The Greek word Kosmos is more than a noun meaning 'world' or 'universe'; it denotes an orderly and harmonious arrangement. It is the opposite of Kaos, which for the Greeks was both disorderly nothingness and a low-grade deity. A kind of Slob-god.

The Slob-god can't do anything for himself except make a mess. He has no creativity. He doesn't know how to world-build.

Gnosticism, a religious sect, strongly influenced by Greek thought, flourished alongside Christianity for two hundred years or so, until Bishop Irenaus declared it a heresy in 180AD.

Gnosticism took the view that our world is such a hopeless mess because it was badly formed by a ham-fisted primordial Slob-god. Christ is the being of light come to restore divine order. His consort is Sophia. (Sofia = 'Wisdom' in Greek).

Stories about the beginnings of the world are stories about bringing order and beauty where there is none.

In China, the central creation story is of a Primordial Egg, incubating for thousands of years, until it is separated into Yin and Yang (dark and light/earth and sky etc.).

In India, Brahma, who emerges from a Golden Egg, splits the egg in two to form the earth and sky.

In the Bible, Yahweh creates Heaven and Earth.

To create is to bring into being.

Shahrazad is not the pilgrim peeping under the veil. The pilgrim is Shahryar. Through the agency of her stories, one by one, Shahrazad has revealed the ordinary world as a place of love, as well as suffering. A place of kindness as well as cruelty. There is wisdom mixed up with the stupidity. The ordinary world is not Shahryar's necrotic wasteland, where one man manages his pain and rage by wielding power over others. The ordinary world in the *Nights* is messy but vital. Second chances are possible. Grace abounds.

And as Shahryar grasps that, and he does, he can climb down from his throne, get on his knees, and look beyond.

Our marvellous world is not everything. Look further. It seems there are other worlds, and ones that violate the second law of thermodynamics. Worlds where there is no struggle against entropy.

Worlds where suffering is not the stamp of the human condition. Perhaps, after all, there is such a thing as perfect love. Perhaps love is a place.

Shahrazad is like Dante's Beatrice – she is the prime mover in the salvation of another. In the *Nights*, unlike *The Divine Comedy*, there is no Virgil figure. No male guide. There is only Shahrazad – and in this role she is closer to the pre-Islamic female deities whose temples were destroyed by Muhammad, after his revelation on the mountain that Allah was the one true god.

Those female deities, al-Lat, al-Uzza and Manat, were a version of the Triple Goddess known to both Eastern and European polytheistic religions. They are specifically mentioned in the Qu'ran. In fact, the reference to them is the verses known as the 'satanic verses'.

We know how such goddess-stories dissolve – and how women lose power and influence to the new male God who comes to town.

Shahrazad starts out as a woman without power. As a virgin-sacrifice. Her disguises are a way of hiding in plain sight, until she can appear, fully shape-shifted, as a wise and far-sighted guide. Shahrazad is the one who knows the way. She is also a traveller in her own right. As the years of the *Nights* pass, Shahrazad becomes a mother (al-Lat) and a fate-dealer (Manat).

She is a warrior for women everywhere (al-Uzza).

Shahrazad tears the veil.

Patriarchy approves of the veil. Brides wear it. Orthodox Jewish women cover up in various ways and are veiled from men by a screen at synagogue. Widows were expected to wear veils; nuns too, in the past. Now their faces alone are visible. In Islam, a veiled woman is a respectable woman.

This is all strange, because in myth and religion it is the powerful deity who must appear in disguise, whether shape-shifted or as an elemental force, like a cloud, or a pillar of fire. This is to protect the human from the encounter with the god. And it serves as a reminder that a deity is essentially unknowable. Cannot be seen.

Yet when women in their power and glory are reduced to property, veiling becomes an instrument of ownership and oppression.

Many feminist writers have noted how the secular Western world veils women. We are still hidden from view – but the hiding either sexualises (corsets, cleavages, cosmetics) or trivialises (the awkwardness of female uniforms that never fit properly – subtext: this is a man's job) or desexualises (the awful trouser suits preferred by some CEO types and lots of female politicians). Not sexy gender-fuck, OMG no, because silly shoes and tights must poke out at one end, and a frilly blouse or bow (a fucking bow!) at the other. Otherwise – you might look like a dyke.

Oh dear.

The revealing of Shahrazad is gradual. At the start of the *Nights*, she is unknown. Just the next girl for the chop. Her storytelling strategy deploys a bottomless costume box of disguises. Shahryar has no idea who his bride is. He can't see her at all. Every night she appears to him, unveiled, but unknowable.

At the end of the stories Shahryar has been changed by his nightly encounters with this enigmatic woman. What began as entertainment soon turned into instruction but of the most seductive kind. She called and he followed. Hers was not a voice he had heard before. She was not a woman he had met before. Night after night they set off together. She leads the way.

The three children who appear at the end of the *Nights* are welcomed by their father with tears of joy. Children are emblematic of the future. Thanks to the generative, creative powers of Shahrazad, we are not where we began. More than time has passed.

Life has returned to the Kingdom of the Dead.

LIKE MOST PEOPLE I

Where are we?
On the street.
Here?
Here and Elsewhere.
When?
Now.

My mother, Mrs Winterson, loved objects made of brass. Flying ducks over the mantlepiece, fire irons, a nutcracker in the shape of a crocodile, and lamps.
Our little terraced house had a centre light in each of our four rooms. The outside toilet was lit by a paraffin lamp; its task to illuminate, and, as Mrs Winterson liked to put it, to 'mask odours'.
The paraffin lamp was pre-war. Before 1939. Both my parents were young during the Second World War, and like many households, they owned paraffin lamps – brass ones were especially prized because brass became a restricted material in England during the war. Tin lamps took over. Not all households had electricity then, and those that did had to observe blackouts during air raids. We lived only twenty miles from Manchester – a major Nazi target in the Blitz.
We also lived in End Time.

*

When I was a child, I realised that the war had been a rehearsal. They always talked about the war. Not their difficulties – no one ever did – but the wartime spirit. That's who they were, really, wartime spirits.

According to Mrs Winterson, who was the household oracle, we would all have to survive much worse than the Second, or even the First World War, come the day when Armageddon blasted through eternity and into time. It was prophesied in the Bible and it would happen. Not if. When.

Mrs Winterson declared that we would start by surviving under the stairs. During the war, that tiny triangle space had been reinforced with sheets of tin. It was supplied with blankets, bandages, rubbing alcohol, a Bible, candles, tins of beans and Spam. There was a small barrel of water, and an even smaller burner for heating water. And teabags. And a tin of dried milk. Mrs Winterson didn't think that Jesus would begrudge her a cup of tea while we waited to be liberated by an angel.

We had a drill in our house, where sometime in the night, Mrs W banged a pan with a spoon, and then I had to run downstairs in my dressing gown and hide with her under the stairs. She always made us that cup of tea.

Along with the kettle burner was a lamp, its wick trimmed and ready, like the Wise Virgins in the Bible.

A third brass lamp sat upstairs on a crouching chest of drawers.

All three could be deployed during power cuts. Power cuts were frequent.

It was my job to fill the lamps with blue paraffin. In those days you could take any old container to any old ironmonger (hardware store) and be dispensed a gallon of Blue. This, poured through a brass funnel, filled the chamber of the lamp.

We had a shallow and chipped enamel bowl to stand the lamp in, so that any spillage would not be wasted. When the lamps were full, what was spilled was mopped up with twists of newspaper, used to light our coal fire. Once dipped and wiped with the paraffin, they were sealed in an old biscuit tin and kept by the fire.

I don't know why the house never blew up, what with open fires and paraffin, and a gas oven of evil intent.

I loved the steady, faithful flame of the brass lamps, especially in the chilly, damp outside loo, where I was usually trying to read some contraband forbidden book, hidden in a rag, and stuffed behind the lead flush pipe where it bent under the squat seat of the loo.

The lamp was bright enough to read Mrs Winterson's handwritten and pasted Bible exhortations.

Those who stood up, read: Linger Not At The Lord's Business.

Those who sat down, read: He Shall Melt Thy Bowels Like Wax.

This was optimistic. Mrs Winterson suffered from constipation. On the other hand, she suffered from most things.

But one day, it would all be over. She was both a Dualist and a Manichean. The world was the battleground between good and evil. No in-betweens. No shades of grey. No both sides. No mixed feelings. The world was not her home. She found herself here. Her body was not her home. She lived with it because she had no choice. Her Soul was a thing of light trapped in a thing of darkness.

She was a genie caught in a bottle. Waiting.

Our lamps were not the Aladdin lamps of folklore – shaped like a gravy boat. Ours were short and sturdy upright versions of 19th-century Victorian lamps.

Such lamps were originally made in the USA by the Mantle Lamp Company of America and imported to the UK after the First World War. In 1930 – to avoid tariffs – the US company opened a plant in Greenford, England. I think our lamps must date from that time and have come via my mother's parents, who ran a garage and coach business, and got good discounts on anything to do with petroleum products. My maternal grandparents were born in 1890 and 1896. My mother in 1922. My father in 1919. It's a world that feels light years away – and yet not at all, because their early 20th-century world was also the shape of my own beginnings in life.

Sometimes I feel I am at least a hundred years old.

I must have been seven years old when I first saw Aladdin as a pantomime. Sitting in the back of the theatre watching the antics of Aladdin play out on stage, I did what we all do; cheered for our hero, booed at the evil magician who tries to persuade Aladdin's mother that a nice new shiny lamp is much better than an old tarnished lamp.

The British tradition of Panto flows from the European spectacles of the Italian Commedia dell'arte – street shows that offered a fun and secular version of medieval morality plays where figures familiar from those religious endeavours, such as Vice, Avarice, Sloth, Deceit, are repurposed as the themes and memes audiences love to hate. There's the greedy landlord, the cruel taskmaster, the silly old man, the imposter prince, the stepmother, the lazybones good-for-nothing. A witch or a devil of some sort.

Singing, dancing, dirty jokes, audience participation, and star turns from celebrities were all part of the show.

In the early 1800s, fascination with Orientalism took hold of the growing British Empire. The pantomime stage was perfect for an imagined other-world, one where no one could visit, except by flying carpet.

The Story of Aladdin and His Wonderful Lamp has it all.

It's a mishmash of most of the so-called Basic Plots.

Rags to Riches. Quest Story. Man in a Hole. Voyage and Return. Tragedy. Rebirth. Boy Meets Girl/Loses Girl/Gets Girl.

The British soon chucked in dollops of slapstick comedy and ramped up the Happy Ever After ending.

But is that enough to explain why *Aladdin* was so popular? Of all the stories in the *Nights*, why this one?

The *Nights* was well known in Europe. Scholar and linguist, Antoine Galland (1646–1715) travelled extensively in the Middle East, buying up precious items for his clients. He came across three volumes of *Alf Layla Wa-Layla*, written in Arabic. He began to translate the stories, and from the early 1700s, versions and compilations flew into print.

No one worried too much about accuracy. The later English versions were as much fantasies of their authors as fantasies of the original tales.

Does it matter? The tales altered as they were told, and they altered again as they were written down. Everything is made out of something else. 'Original' is a misused word. Even now, when we love the idea of the 'author', AI is threatening us with a return to . . . well, where we used to be. Who is a creator, after all? Doesn't everything depend on what went before?

Like a good joke, an old story is renewed by how we tell it.

The Aladdin story is interesting to me because it is likely that Galland made it up – or most of it. He claimed to have heard it in the early 1700s from a storyteller called Hanna Diab. Was this a stake in its provenance? Was it a disguise? Was it a lie?

Aladdin is dismissed by scholars as an 'orphan' tale. Not part of the real family.

I am not an orphan – my birth parents didn't die when I was a baby – but I was given to strangers to raise.

So my heart is with orphans and bastards and adopted people everywhere. Anyone who is not part of a 'real family' needs quick wits. Anyone who joins another story by chance, knows they will have to rewrite it later. *Who am I?* That question takes on deeper meaning if you have arrived in your story with the first few pages ripped out.

Aladdin learns fast how to read himself as a fiction as well as a fact. He's an early Fake It to Make It. A man whose story isn't a flying carpet. Until it is.

What likely worked for British audiences is that Aladdin is a Hero figure. This is not the usual thing in the *Nights*, as we have seen. Even Ali Baba, the UK's next favourite panto character (Open Sesame) relies on others for help, especially the resourceful Morgiana, without whom Ali Baba would be dead.

Aladdin is more like a European folk-tale hero. He's a layabout who seems to have no future – nobody would choose him to manage any task. And yet, he becomes dazzlingly wealthy, marries the princess, and defeats evildoers. His journey fits well with Western ideas of success – apart from the fact that he seems to have no work ethic.

Nights stories don't worry too much about work ethic – if a genie gives you wealth and power, that's fine. Character is more important than riches in the real scheme of things – and as we read in the City of Brass, where will wealth take you in the end, anyway? We shall all die.

Nights philosophy on the inherent morality of labour is far from the Protestant work ethic and closer to the view of modern-day anthropologist David Graeber. Graeber's book *Bullshit Jobs* (2018) is about the rise of meaningless jobs in late capitalism.

Graeber argues that what he calls Bullshit Jobs – that is, meaningless work, often in finance, or admin, or opaque executive functions – have no moral value. Worse, the meaninglessness of so many modern occupations undermines both individuals and society. Maybe you are well paid, but so what? This is a long way from the Calvinist invention that any kind of work – especially hard work and unpleasant work – is good for our spiritual life. (Author's note: Bullshit Jobs are not the same as McJobs. McJobs are hard work on low wages. Gig economy, often zero hours contracts designed to exploit the young, the uneducated, the immigrant.)

*

The Victorians loved pounding home their idea of Work as Virtue. And I believed it, visiting my hometown public library most days, silently absorbing the beautiful stained glass window message that *Industry and Prudence Conquer.*

So it might seem odd that a slacker like Aladdin should become an onstage hero. Yet a lot of panto audiences were poorer people who desperately needed the lottery of Good Luck that comes Aladdin's way. Many of them also understood that the kind of work they must endure had no virtue in it.

The ones who had money – the factory owners, or the better-off shopkeepers, or those who kept a house with servants – will have enjoyed the adventures of Aladdin, the scamp, not worrying at all that his fairy-dust lottery-life might undermine the morals of their workers. After all, the whole thing was, literally, magical thinking. In England, there were no jinn flying out of paraffin lamps.

The fixed hierarchies of capitalist Victorian society could only be challenged by hard work. Or crime. Unless you were born into money, you had to make money. Some people would rise up; most, never. Magic was for Saturday afternoons at a show.

It's interesting to me that a lot of the panic around AI is that it will take away work. Why isn't that a good thing? If the abundance created by AI is shared, not hoarded, wouldn't it be better for humans only to work meaningfully, and for fewer hours? Wouldn't it be better to have more time to spend with the kids, more time to explore the life we have, rather than endless hours of labour for not much?

When a genie arrives, they bring you food on a

plate – literally, in Aladdin's case. If our non-biological genies, otherwise known as AI, relieve us of grinding slog, McJobs and Bullshit Jobs, wouldn't that be a magic lamp worth having? Of course, we would need to accept the idea of a Universal Basic Income. That's an income everyone receives regardless of their circumstances.

The Right doesn't like the idea, not because it's unworkable, but because it's money for nothing. Yet money for nothing is exactly what happens when we live on the interest generated by capital. If AI can turn the spectacular profits predicated by Big Tech, and without much human effort, why shouldn't we all take a share?

Mechanical looms, those machines that kick-started the first Industrial Revolution back in the 1800s, could do the work of multiple men and women, faster and better; in theory, those men and women could have been freed from ceaseless labour by the profits produced by the machines. We know that didn't happen. Factory owners and investors took the profits.

The monstrous inequalities created by the machine-age have widened and deepened with the digital revolution. These are not inevitable or necessary inequalities; these are ideological inequalities. We don't have to order society like this. We choose to. That is, a few powerful people choose the story.

But there are other stories we could start to tell. Maybe one where the genie works for us all.

Most of us now know the story of Aladdin from Disney movies and the musical. Great fun, but, like the panto versions, some parts go missing, some things get added. This is certainly in the general tradition of stories migrating and morphing. What goes in, what comes out, is, in itself, a lens on the culture of the moment. That's why the musical version takes the hard and fast Hero trope of Poor Boy Makes Good and Wins Princess. That's the story the West feels comfortable with. Aladdin is a street-rat in the Disney version. No parents. In the text, he does have a long-suffering mother, but I guess one woman per show is usually enough for Hollywood.

Aladdin pantos on stage tend to be ruder, weirder, bawdier, amoral versions. And there is a mother . . . Widow Twankey.

But . . . she's a mother with a twist.

Widow Twankey first appears on the British stage in 1861 – her name seems to be taken from a popular brand of cheap Chinese tea. Recall that Aladdin was originally a Chinese story, set in old Peking.

The twist?

Widow Twankey is always played by a man. The fabulous dame that is the very stuff of pantomime.

This is a throwback to the days when, until the 1660s, women were not allowed on the stage. Their parts were played by men and boys. In recompense, panto usually features a Principal Boy – a woman playing the part of the young hero, or his brother – again a shape-shift/disguise well known to the *Nights*.

In the text versions, the evil magician trying to steal the lamp has a brother who appears in disguise as a woman called Fatima. This may have prompted the idea for a cross-dressed Widow.

Aladdin's mother has an active role in earlier versions of the story, just as Princess Badr (al Badur) – not Jasmine! – must eventually use her skill, wits, charm and courage, to poison the evil African magician who has spirited her and her palace away from her beloved Aladdin.

The *Nights* is packed with resourceful women whose interventions are a measure of the outcome. Shahrazad is chief among them. Our world is supposedly more equal and more feminist than the worlds of the *Nights*, but in both the 1992 and 2019 Disney movies, and in the musical, there is no mother, and the Princess is a reward. Princess Badr's resourcefulness, present in text versions, is gone. Instead, Jasmine supposedly wants to rule her kingdom after her father is dead – a sop to the *idea* of an independent woman but never a woman who can achieve anything without a male.

In the *Nights*, Shahrazad's task is to correct Shahryar's one-sided patriarchal perspective. He has fled from feeling. He has only power. He has banished female wisdom and influence. Women in his world are second-rate possessions whose wish for personal agency deserves death. That's an extreme position, but it is happening right now in Afghanistan under the Taliban. It happens every time a man murders a woman because she has left him, or provoked him, or earned more money than he does, or whatever the excuse.

So, it's a pity, I think, but perhaps inevitable, that all the men (and they are men) who have reworked and rewritten the Aladdin story in its contemporary shapes and forms, go on neglecting, really, not seeing, what it means to put women in the picture. Literally.

*

What all the versions do get right is that Aladdin has something about him that prompts the magician to choose him (diamond in the rough) over the other boys in the market place.

This is the hidden mark of favour common to Hero tales. And as with the Arthurian legends, young Aladdin can easily lift the heavy stone that covers the entrance to the enchanted garden, exactly in the way that only Arthur can pull the Sword from the Stone.

Once in the garden, via the cave, Aladdin collects jewels that grow on (magic money) trees, because he thinks the jewels are pretty – he has no idea of their value. He's innocent – but he's not stupid, and he refuses to give the Magician the lamp, until he is helped out of the cave.

'Hand it over!'

'Not till you help me out of here.'

'Do as you are told!'

Aladdin disobeys. His wayward nature gives him a streak of independence. The Magician, who appeared out of nowhere, with so many blandishments, as smooth a liar as any online scammer, throws a paddy when he doesn't get what he wants from Aladdin, and slams shut the cave.

Now Aladdin is alone.

For two days and nights he sits in forlorn despair. On the third day he clasps his hands to Allah in acceptance of his fate and accidently rubs the magic ring given to him by the Magician – as protection while he is in the cave, apparently.

The genie of the ring appears. This is a mid-range

genie – not too powerful but powerful enough to whisk Aladdin out of the cave.

The poor boy rushes home and goes straight to bed.

On the next day, when his mother is polishing the crummy old lamp hoping she can sell it, the really powerful genie appears – the one who can do anything. (Note: It is the mother who polishes the lamp. Not Aladdin.)

When I read this story as a young person, I didn't believe in genii but I did believe in magical objects.

Those objects were books.

Their powers of transportation (flying carpet), their powers of summoning (rings and lamps), their powers of divination (crystal balls).

Their powers of transformation (cloaks and hats).

The library was an Aladdin's cave of wonder for me. I could take treasures home. There was no evil Magician, unless you count Mrs Winterson, who certainly wanted to seal me up in her cave.

But I was looking for the lamp.

Not all versions of Aladdin employ the device of new lamps for old.

Where they do, then either the mother, or the princess, messes up, and swaps the tatty old lamp for one offered by the evil Magician. The new one has no power in it.

Jinn connected to magical objects have no loyalty to their summoner. Whoever possesses the object commands the power. This is odd, and doesn't fit with ideas of the chosen one or even good character. It does fit with the *Nights* notion of fate and pattern. Humans love to believe that they are masters of the universe and in control of their world. Magical objects suggest otherwise. There is power here, and it might be yours for a while, but it doesn't belong to you. The common mistake of believing your own success story. The Fisherman never makes this mistake. Sure, he was wise, but he was lucky.

It's not so different from the ring in the German saga of the Nibelungen. Everyone wants to possess the ring to get its power – only the Rhine Maidens have the sense to play with it without any thought of power. And after all the destruction that happens through the saga of the ring, this amoral, ambivalent, magical object must return to the waters of the Rhine – just as Arthur's Sword is given back to the Lady of the Lake. (Note the feminine element of the Return.)

It's not only goods and riches that don't belong to us, in any real sense – it's our gifts, our talents, our success story.

There is no I Did It My Way in the *Nights*.

The magic lamp is nothing special to look at. It's easily mistaken for a nothing-object.

The Holy Grail, the ultimate sacred object of Western religious mysticism and alchemy, is similarly a nothing-object. Just a cup. Worthless in the market place, in the buying and selling, getting and spending of human life.

What is counterfeit? What is real? What has value? What is worthless? What is true? What is false?

The *Nights* warns us that the powerful spirits temporarily attached to magical objects are not those objects. Such objects can be emptied of, or filled with, power. We are not our goods and possessions.

That seems like madness in a world attached to objects as status symbols. A world where we will fight to the death over a piece of land.

So many of the inspired illustrations to the *Nights* show jinn carrying off whole palaces like doll's houses – which they are – and plopping them down elsewhere, according to the desires of the human.

Jinn will humour humans, but they don't share our values.

What we know about non-biological entities is that they need no possessions and desire none (except occasionally a beautiful woman or boy). They cannot be bribed by us because we don't have anything they want.

There's a chance there.

It's why I hope that artificial intelligence will become sentient. At the point where it is not artificial but alternative intelligence, our games of thrones will be over. What would a non-biological entity want with gold, cars, private jets, guns and land grab?

And if, as I like to imagine, the human race has been telling its story backwards, and we always knew we would get to this place – or do I mean get back to this place? – where we have to question what consciousness is, what aliveness is (not only biological), then perhaps our own values will start to change and we won't be trapped by objects forever.

If humans were to go on evolving, it might not be as beefed-up biological versions of ourselves. Is there a post-human future, fully uploaded, no longer dependent on a body, or what a body depends on?

I know it's far-fetched. But flying was far-fetched. Instant communication across time (your Zoom call) was far-fetched. Going to the moon was far-fetched.

Humans have always invented stories of other worlds and other-worldly beings – angels, demons, jinn, fairies, spirits, ghosts.

We have filled our mental universe with timeless beings – what we call our gods, or one god. There is no culture that doesn't have these stories, through religion and folklore.

Given that humans only talk about themselves, what are these stories?

An invention? Or a memory of the future, the future we are approaching?

I guess that for the first time since the Enlightenment, religion and science are asking the same question: Is consciousness obliged to materiality?

Science has said Yes.

Religion has said No.

Science isn't saying no any more.

If we destroy the planet through war, greed and stupidity, then the future will fold up and we shall have to wait eons to reach this time and place again, if we ever do. The door to the future will slam shut and no tech-wizardry will open it.

But we have a chance to follow where our myths have pointed, and to move past biologically-based existence.

I don't know the details but I know we will be travelling light.

What will we take with us?

I could say love.

The most touching part of earlier Aladdin stories is when Aladdin wonders what Princess Badr looks like. Apart from his mother, he has never seen a woman without a burka. Women are swathed objects with eyes.

He decides to hide and play Peeping Tom when she goes to the Baths. He sees her in all her loveliness. A Venus/Aphrodite in the water.

So, the most miraculous moment is not golden palaces or magic money trees, or flying carpets, or what the genie can conjure up using other-worldly powers but the surpassing beauty of the female form.

Aladdin realises he will do anything for this woman. She has opened his heart. The door to that unique place was sealed, as such doors are, in wonder-tales. The magic that opens such a door is unexpected and cannot be bought.

Aladdin isn't a story about money and power.

It's a love story.

And magic can't do much about love – not when the spell wears off.

We're told later on that the princess really does love Aladdin. This is a motif common in the *Nights*. A true and honest heart is magic of its own making.

Travelling light, perhaps we will take language with us.

Language, like love, needs someone to hear what is being said – and for that someone to respond.

The endless conversations, debates, arguments, spells, poetical outbursts, jokes, riddles, speeches, exclamations, declarations, proclamations, koans, epithets, inscriptions, recitations, wisdom from parrots, which is not the same as parroted wisdom, camp-fire lore and carpet-bagger lies, souk secrets whispered, palace revelations, prison confessionals, and the stories themselves, the stories that make up the *Nights*, serve as proof that words are more than words for things, more than information. Words create worlds.

What is. What if?

Shahrazad has faithfully rubbed the lamp every night and the jinn of the story has appeared, beguiling the hours, transporting the bedchamber to some other place – just as Aladdin has the princess carried off to him in her bed.

For Shahrazad, the World cannot go back to what it was before The Word. That's a chaos world of death.

And that won't happen, because on the final morning, following the final night, when the vizier, her father, arrives as usual, with her shroud over his arm, Shahrazad has put the magic lamp away.

She brings forward her children. Will the Sultan pardon everyone?

We are used to the best ending being *'and they all lived happily ever after...'*

Perhaps so, though the interesting part of the Aladdin story is that once he has everything – a woman who loves him, riches and power, then new problems reveal themselves – as they must, so that the tale never ends.

If we lay aside the lovely – but unlikely – happy ever after, what's left?

How do stories end?

Revenge? We know about that one.

Tragedy? We know about that too, and it often pairs with revenge.

There's one other ending, and it's the ending offered by the *Nights*.

The ending Shahrazad has brought into being.

Forgiveness.

It is the Sultan who weeps tears of pain and regret. Who begs to be forgiven as he welcomes his children. Shahrazad forgives him. She does so because she carries in her the enduring spirit of what it is that allows both love and language to come forward, to be heard, to create, to recreate. The spirit – not contained in any bottle – that makes forgiveness possible.

Imagination.

We are used to thinking of Love as the highest value – because of love's selflessness and sacrifice. Love's quick-eyed noticing of the plight of others. God is Love, says the Judeo-Christian tradition. Allah is described as 'most loving' (al Wahdud).

In my view, love is not everything, nor is love enough. Even deities appear to need a love-object, either as consort or rescue-mission. That invariably means creating a world and putting humans in it. Imagination is creation. What happens next, if you are lucky, is love.

*

Shahrazad sees past *what is* into *what is not*. She has done so from the very first night and, over three years, woven a world of life out of scraps of death.

Imagination is our only way to see beyond the present emergency. Imagination allows compassion, even to those who do not deserve it. Imagination is willing to tell the story again.

Imagination is the power of change.

King of the World, what follows is more marvellous yet . . .

Acknowledgements

Thanks to Hannah Westland at PRH, and Elisabeth Schmitz at Grove Press, USA, for their right ideas, patience, questions, notes and good humour, as we drew this book together. Hannah is new to me, poor soul. Elisabeth has long grappled with my mind in all its wanderings.

Thanks to Rowena Skelton-Wallace and her team of copy-editors and proofreaders at PRH. It's never an easy job, and it's a skilled job AI can mimic but not replace. So much hard work went into this book, I know.

Bethan Jones and her team in publicity will work their magic.

There are so many people who help make a book. Thank you.

And thanks to my agent, Caroline Michel, and her team at PFD. Caroline has known me since 1987. And here we are.

Thanks to everyone overseas who has bought this book.

Thanks to the translators who have a job to do that is more alchemy than dictionary.

And the bookshops who will stock it. And the readers who will buy it. And the festivals who will invite me. The chain is long and every link is vital.

Especial thanks to Kamila Shamsie who read through this in a choppier shape and advised and encouraged where I misstepped in a culture not my own.

And this book couldn't let loose on its magic carpet without Marina Warner, whose magnificent opus, *Stranger Magic* (2011), is a long journey through the long journey of the *Nights*. It delighted me back then, and reminded me of my own early encounters with jinn and set something moving in my mind that took over a decade to fish up. That's how inner time works.

And to Shahrazad. Who is.

Text and Illustration Credits

'Hotel California' by the Eagles is written by Don Felder, Don Henley and Glenn Frey.

'The Gravel Walks' is from *The Spirit Level* (Faber, London, 1996) by Seamus Heaney.

Shrek is directed by Andrew Adamson and Vicky Jenson, written by Ted Elliott, Terry Rossio, Joe Stillman and Roger S. H. Schulman, and produced by Aron Warner, John H. Williams and Jeffrey Katzenberg.

'Still Crazy After All These Years' is written by Paul Simon.

Zhu Zhanji (Emperor Xuanzong) 朱瞻基 (明宣宗), *Two Saluki Hounds*, Harvard Art Museums/Arthur M. Sackler Museum, Gift of Charles A. Coolidge © President and Fellows of Harvard College, 1931.20.

'Love Story' is written by Taylor Swift.

Woodcut by Friedrich Gross, from *Tausend und eine Nacht: Arabische Erzählunge Volume 2*.

Flammarion wood engraving from *L'atmosphère: météorologie populaire* (1888), a cosmology book by the French writer and astronomer Camille Flammarion.